I0691394

Clydesdale

GOES TO A FUNERAL

First Edition

Published by The Nazca Plains Corporation
Las Vegas, Nevada
2010

ISBN: 978-1-935509-70-7

Published by

The Nazca Plains Corporation ®
4640 Paradise Rd, Suite 141
Las Vegas NV 89109-8000

PUBLISHER'S NOTE
Clydesdale Goes to a Funeral is a work of fiction created wholly
by *Bob Archman*'s imagination. All characters are fictional and any
resemblance to any persons living or deceased is purely by accident.
No portion of this book reflects any real person or events.

Cover Photos,
Christopher Howey and Christopher Weigl

Art Director,
Blake Stephens

Clydesdale

GOES TO A FUNERAL

First Edition

Bob Archman

Part I

Mom always jokingly asked why no one ever killed her sister Edith. Her sister, my Aunt Edith, had a special ability to enrage and insult. She had been pretty as a girl, but my Aunt Ellen said, Edith hadn't aged, she soured. She married late and tried to make up for her increasingly unattractive appearance by being exceptionally narrow and intolerant of anything she regarded as "sinful", "immoral" or "modern."

While she was expert at finding sin in the most ordinary and simple of human endeavors, Edith's sense of virtues didn't seem to include charity, tolerance, love, or affection. She was attracted to crackpot preachers and to sanctimonious freeloaders. This got her in trouble several times, especially after Uncle Edgar died. Edgar was by no means a catch, but he could spot a con man two counties away.

It was ten in the morning when Mom called me and said Edith was dead. Mom wanted me to come right away. "I think there is something wrong," she said.

"What can be more wrong than dead?" I asked.

"I don't know exactly. Your Aunt Becky called. She didn't want to talk on the phone," Mom replied.

Fortunately, things were quiet at Clydesdale & Company, my security agency. By noon, I was on the way home. It was a long drive to southwest Virginia and Mom called me on the cell phone three times. The first time was to say Edith had been murdered. Then she called to say the body had been mutilated, and finally to say Edith's house had been torched.

By the time I got home, Mom was frantic. Her sisters were coming and I was to take them immediately to Wythetown, Edith's hometown. Wythetown was the county seat of Talliaferro County. Talliaferro was one of Virginia's western most Counties. It was noted for its poverty and inaccessibility. It was mountainous, with poor roads and with few resources, other than a particularly poor grade of coal.

Talliaferro, pronounced Tolliver, had been briefly prosperous at the turn of the twentieth century. There were several coalmines that had once employed several thousand men. The coal produced as little heat and as much soot as was possible and after World War I the mines were abandoned for cleaner fuel sources.

At 74, Mom was the youngest of the sisters. Becky was 77 and Ellen 80. They were spry, but the drive west was too much for them, especially considering the famously poor state of roads in parts of rural Virginia. My Aunts arrived just after I got there. We transferred my bag to Ellen's Buick 88 and left for Wythetown. It was a long five hours before we arrived at Edith's burned out house.

A policeman was on guard. Becky went up to him to get information. I'm pretty sure he wasn't supposed to tell us what he did, but Becky had her ways. Becky had been a High School Latin teacher. She was noted for being firm, but fair and she was every inch a lady. Becky expected people to tell her what she wanted to know. The Policeman, Officer

Rollie Watterson, was a well mannered country boy and he told her as many details as he knew.

Firemen discovered the body after they put out the fire. "It was a poor attempt at a fire," Rollie said. "More smoke than flame. At first they thought it was a typical smoking in bed thing."

"Edith didn't smoke," Ellen said.

"That what one of the guys in the Fire Department said," Rollie said. "Scooter had her for Sunday School. He said, "Miss Edith didn't smoke, didn't drink and hardly took a breath without asking the Lord's permission. Scooter smelled something fishy from the start."

"When they found the body, they knew something was really wrong," Rollie continued. "There were parts missing." Becky gasped. "Sorry ma'am, maybe I shouldn't have said that."

"Not at all," Mom chimed in. "I'm a nurse and not squeamish at all. Please tell us all." He continued. It was getting dark and a red truck drove up. A skinny guy with a huge handlebar mustache got out. Somehow, I guessed it was Scooter. I was right.

"I was just driving by and saw you guys here, what's up Rollie?" he asked. He sounded authoritative and mad.

"These are Miss Edith's folks, Scooter," Rollie replied, "her sisters and a nephew."

Scooter's attitude changed immediately, "Sorry about your loss," he said. "It's a bad situation. Miss Edith's body is at the medical examiners, so you'll have some time to make arrangements." We talked more about the events surrounding Edith's death. By now it was dark and it was getting cold. In the dim light, I could see Aunt Ellen was shivering.

"I think I'd better get the ladies to a motel," I said. "This has been a shock to them."

"The motel situation here is poor," Rollie said. "The Town and Country has seen better days."

"Well, as long as it clean," Mom said.

"Clean is kind of the problem, ma'am," Rollie said. "It's not too good for ladies. Even the Mexicans don't think much of it."

"My Mom has a room, if you don't mind things being a bit down home," Scooter said.

Rollie laughed. "Scooter's Mom is a nice lady, not like Scooter at all," he said. "It's a pretty house." My Aunts thought that would be fine. Scooter called his mother and she said she'd get the room ready. Scooter bumped into to me accidentally. I didn't react. A little later he bumped into me again, this time not by accident.

"The boy here can bunk with me," Scooter said. "I've got a double-wide on the other side of the farm." I wanted to find out more, but Mom and her sisters were worn out. I followed Scooter into the countryside and then down a long farm road. The moon was out and the farmhouse was impressive. It was a two-story stone building with all the lights on.

Scooter's mother greeted us at the door. It took at least thirty seconds for Mom and her sisters to realize Scooter's mother, Elizabeth, was a like spirit. Ellen was looking a bit shaky. Elisabeth produced tea and a cake. She was sympathetic and had the ability to appear to be effortlessly helpful.

Scooter said he had to get up early with the cows, so we went off. I left the Buick at the house, and drove in his pickup. He said the road wasn't Buick friendly.

His double wide was a half mile away. It was a big farm. "I'm ready for a beer," Scooter said. "Are you a drinking man?"

"A beer sounds great."

He got out a Miller. "Your folks don't seem much like Miss Edith," he said cautiously.

"Thank you Jesus," I said. "Aunt Edith was a problem. Mom and my other aunts are normal. We never figured out what got into Edith."

Scooter smiled. "She was a trip. I hated her in Sunday school. She was a mean as they come, but as I got older I got to think of her as a type," Scooter said. "My Mom tries to think the best of people, but even she admitted Miss Edith was a challenge." We talked for a while and had another beer.

I remembered the bumps in the dark and decided to go for it. "What in hell do you do for entertainment here? You're a long way from the big city lights."

"Other than satellite television?" he asked with a sly smile on his face.

"You got some buddies?"

"A few," he said. "Fishing buddies, hunting buddies, fire department buddies. You've got friends?"

"Sure," I said. "Mostly fuck buddies."

Scooter laughed. "That's my favorite kind."

"I need to warn you, I'm 90% a top."

"I'd guess I'm 50/50." Scooter said. He was 6" taller than I was and he was looking at me in frank appraisal.

"Are you the kind of guy who likes to know someone before he gets down and dirty?" I asked.

"Shit, if there's a cock involved, I don't even need to see a guy's face," Scooter said as he unbuttoned his shirt.

"A romantic?" I said as I stripped.

He nodded, and then laughed, "Sure, I'm romantic as hell." By now, he was shirtless. He was thin, but quite muscular. He had taken off his baseball cap and was balding, but what he lacked on his head he made up for on his chest. The mat of dirty blond chest hair linked to his bush with a treasure trail. His cock was long and uncut. His nuts hung low in a hairy ball sack.

"Damn, you're a fucking gorilla," he exclaimed just before I dropped my pants. He whistled.

"You said you bottomed?" I asked.

Scooter looked at me a bit sheepishly. "I don't know about that. If I'd seen the coming attractions I might not have volunteered that information," he said as he stared at my cock. "I sure do like what I'm seeing. Your dick must be half your body weight."

"Don't worry Scooter, I never stick it where it's not wanted," I said.

"Wanting ain't the problem," Scooter said. I started sucking on his cock. He had what I call an ice teaspoon style cock. It was long and thin, with a bloated cock head at the tip. We were soon sixty-nining on the floor and the curve of his erect organ was a perfect fit for my throat. I could deep throat him and still breathe as his cock head massaged my tonsils. Scooter had a lantern jaw and he came damn close to deep throating me.

Scooter may not have been a romantic, but I knew we were going to hit it off. After a few minutes, he seemed like an old friend. I've never heard anyone talking about a cock as a communication organ, but you can tell. I got Scooter from stop to 100 mph in 40 seconds or less. There was so much pre cum it was almost as if he was ejaculating. I was revved up too.

"Damn Scooter, you can pick them!" a voice said. I jumped, turned over and saw Rollie standing beside us taking off his shirt. Rollie was a black haired bear-like man. He must have been in his twenties and looked as if he still had some baby fat, but he looked good to me.

Scooter must have seen Rollie entering the room. He didn't jump and continued deep throating me. He slowly pulled off, exposing my cock to Rollie for the first time.

"Holy shit!" Rollie exclaimed. I'm good about recognizing all the signs of a size queen. Rollie had twelve of the ten most common signs. I don't think you can get whiplash from getting erect too fast, but Rollie was close. He pushed Scooter out of the way and went after my cock.

Rollie was clean-shaven, balding, and shaved his neck to an inch below his collar. From that line down, he had a pelt. He also had huge balls. As Rollie sucked me, Scooter got off the bed, coated his cock with lube and rear-ended the policeman. Rollie sighed in relief as if a particularly annoying itch was scratched.

"I hope I'm not telling stories out of school, but Rollie here likes the bottom," Scooter said and he slowly thrust his cock into Rollie's ass. "He's not exactly a bottom pig, but he's damn close."

"I take it you boys are old friends?"

"Since we were twelve years old," Scooter said. "Sucking at twelve, fucking at fifteen. Don't worry. We aren't lovers, just pals." Scooter tensed up, then began to twitch. He shuddered and twitched with every ejaculation.

"Sorry about that," he said. "It caught me by surprise. I wasn't expecting it." Scooter looked at me. "Do you have a problem with sloppy seconds?"

"I have no problem if Rollie is okay with it," I answered.

"Don't worry about Rollie. Just think of me as his social secretary," Scooter said. "Just take your time, and he'll be fine." I later found out Rollie had been a linebacker on his high school team and had spent four years in the Marines. He was a firm believer in the no pain no gain school of life.

Rollie had a tight ass, but I used my cock as a battering ram and got in. While I sensed he wanted my cock, he fought it all the way. Once my cock head was on the dark and warm side of his sphincter, Rollie became a whimpering pussycat. I know a number of men who like to be fucked, but Rollie was right up there at the top.

Sperm is the best lube, and Scooter had shot a bucketful of the stuff deep in his rectum. Rollie's sphincter remained tight, forming a natural cock ring. I'm uncut and have some extra skin. The sphincter held the skin, while the shaft and head churned Scooter's cum. If sperm could make butter, we'd have had it.

Rollie didn't last long. He started shooting after five or six minutes of heavy fucking. Since Scooter and Rollie had shot off, I figured I was out of luck. Most guys aren't interested in sex for a while after they've shot.

I miss judged Scooter. He had watched me fuck his pal and wanted to give it a spin himself. "Clydesdale, I'm not sure I can take it, but I'd like to give it a try," he said. "Would you mind if I sat on it?" Needless to say, I said yes.

A half hour later Scooter was skewered on my cock. He'd sit on it and then get up, squirt more lube in his ass then take his seat again. Each time his did this, he'd get another inch in his hole. When about seven inches were in, his eyes crossed. I flipped him over and fucked him on his back. I took my time, but I realized my judgment as to his sexual capacity was better than his.

It was one of those situations when taking my cock was more like climbing Mt. Everest than a real pleasure. Once I was in, I pushed his knees back so they touched his chest and fucked him good. Briefly, I was afraid I had gone too far, but a second later Scooter had a hands free orgasm. Given he'd had a monster orgasm a half hour earlier; I took that as a good sign. I shot off and collapsed on the bed.

I hate to sound tacky, but fucking a guy to the moon and back the first time you meet him is a damn good icebreaker. It's also exciting. I figure once your cock head's on the dark side of a guys sphincter, the getting to know you part of the relationship is a piece of cake. It's a lot better than asking what a guy's sign is. Someone once told me I was a Virgo with a penis rising. The three of us did some express bonding.

When I woke the next morning, Scooter was gone to his cows, but Rollie was still there. He wanted to be fucked again, and we had a good time. He went off to work and I went off to the big house to see what my Mom and Aunts were doing.

They were having breakfast and talking. Miss Elizabeth was fifteen years younger than my Mom, but the same sort of person, sensible self reliant and reasonable. She knew everyone and everything, so she gave guidance to find right undertaker and she knew who ran the cemetery.

Scooter appeared. He had showered and didn't show any signs of the activities with the cows. My Aunts wanted to go to the house. Scooter thought I might be better if he and I went there and scouted it out. Elizabeth agreed with her. She said she would be glad to go with my family to make arrangements. I could check out the house with Scooter. He was the designated arson investigator for the fire department.

There was something unsaid as to why my mother and aunts shouldn't go to Edith's house. As Scooter drove me into town, I asked he what was up.

"The place is a real mess. We're not sure, but some parts of your Aunt may be missing," he explained. "We don't know if they were burned up, or were removed. Some still may be in the house. I think we'd better know before the ladies go looking around the house."

Another volunteer fireman was watching the house as we drove up. The big boys from Roanoke were on their way to do the major forensic investigation. "Arson in these parts is usually burning barns or sheds and 90% of the time it's done by teenagers," Scooter said. "The other 10% is for insurance. I've never been close to having anything like this here."

"Was there an accelerant?"

"I smelled gasoline when I got here," Scooter said. "Given the condition of the body, I'm pretty sure she was dead well before the fire."

We went into the house. The living room, dining room and kitchen were only smoke and water damaged. I recognized some of the furniture as belonging to my grandparents. My Aunt Becky had some parts of the old parlor suite in her house. The china cabinet was undamaged and I saw some of the hand painted china done by my great-grandmother was in there.

The acrid smell of the fire pervaded everything. We went upstairs to the bedroom. The door to the master bedroom was open. The damage was greater here, but it was superficial. The house had plaster ceilings and the fire had not spread into the attic. All the bedding and the mattress were destroyed. The windows were broken out and clear, bright sunlight into the room.

"You can see a lot better today. There was still smoke everywhere yesterday," Scooter remarked. There were odd-looking things here and there. One glob of stuff turned out to be a clock radio. Broken pots held the remains of houseplants. I remembered Edith was known for her green thumb. Next to the pots was an oddly shaped piece of wood. There was something shiny on the wood. When I looked closer, I saw it was a ring, a wedding ring. It took me a few seconds to realize the charred wood was Aunt Edith's hand.

I came really close to throwing up.

Part 2

Aunt Edith wasn't a nice woman, but no one deserves what happened to her. Scooter got me out of the house as the Arson investigators arrived. The Arson group had two large RV type vehicles. One was a mobile lab and the other was an office, command-post unit. A police cruiser followed behind. The Police Chief and a patrolman were in the car. The Police chief was a loud and unpleasant man. Scooter told me the chief was named Willard Thompson. Thompson was mad at Scooter for calling in the Arson unit. Thompson didn't look at Scooter or me and went right to the investigators from Roanoke.

"It's the damn Mexicans," he proclaimed. "They're stealing everything. They're just the kind of people to do this sort of thing."

"Were any Mexicans seen in the area before the fire?" the head investigator asked.

"Of course they were," Chief Thompson said. "They're everywhere."

There was a couple on the porch of the house next door watching the goings on. The man came over to Thompson and the investigator. "I'm Bob Smith, we live next door," he said. "There were no Mexicans in the area yesterday."

"How do you know that?" Thompson asked. He was puffed up and apparently thought he could intimidate the neighbor.

"Sally and I have been outside for most of the daylight hours for the last week," Mr. Smith said, not intimidated one bit. "We were working on our garden. This has been the only good weather we've had for a month. We saw no strangers in the neighborhood." Thompson tried to get them to change their minds but there was no way the Smiths would budge. I liked the Smiths.

An official looking car drove up and three men got out. It was unmarked, but had an impressive array of antennas poking out the rear. The men were dressed in fire department blue. Scooter and I went over to the group. "Sir, I'm Scooter Jones, a member of the fire department," he said introducing himself to the head investigator. "This is Clydesdale Noland, a relative of the victim."

"Are you the guy who called me?" the man asked of Scooter. Scooter nodded. "I'm Captain Donnan." We all shook hands except for Thompson. He didn't join in. Donnan looked at me. "Are you the guy from Richmond?" I nodded. He looked me over, taking a quick look at my basket. "You look just the way they say you do."

"Sorry about that," I replied. He laughed and then got down to business. Donnan knew his stuff. Scooter was a down-home guy, but he gave a good report on the fire. It was simple, direct and consisted only of facts. He was a good observer. Thompson looked on, then turned and left.

"He's an opinionated man," Donnan said as the chief left.

"Asshole," Bob Smith said. "Chief Thompson is an asshole."

"I don't think robbery was the motive," Scooter said. "Clydesdale found a severed hand in the bedroom. The rings were still on it."

"How big was it?" Donnan asked.

"I remember when Uncle Edgar gave it to her for their 40th wedding anniversary," I said. "It caused quite a stir. They said it was two and a half, or three carats."

"Was that the ring you saw?" Donnan asked.

"I think so. It was hard to look," I said. Another attack of nausea came over me. I must have turned green, everyone looked concerned, but I didn't toss my cookies.

Donnan got our phone numbers and asked if we would be available later in the day. We were. Scooter and I went back to the farm. "Thank God Mom and my Aunts weren't there," I said. "That would have been awful if they saw the hand."

"How does Captain Donnan know you?" Scooter asked. I told him about my business in Richmond.

"I know some guys in the Arson Squad there," I said. "I guess the word spread."

"Was he checking you out?" Scooter asked. "How well do you know those guys on the Arson Squad?"

I smiled. "I know one or two really well. You may not believe this, but I'm a good guy to have on an investigation. I'm both helpful and fun to have around."

"I can see that," Scooter said as we drove up to his farmhouse. I hadn't focused on the house the night before, but it was handsome, almost a mansion. It was well maintained and in beautiful shape, surrounded by well-tended gardens. The Buick was there with two other cars.

Inside were my Mom, my Aunts and a minister, the Rev. Mr. John Pettigrew, A second man was dressed like an undertaker. He was an undertaker, Mr. William Graves. Graves looked very somber, but was young and turned out to be a friend of Scooter.

"Your sister was getting ready to join St. John's," Pettigrew said. "I talked with her many times. After her husband died, she seemed to have tried out several local churches, mostly obscure ones. She told me she had been foolish and unkind. She wanted to make peace with God. I told her, she needed to make peace with the people she had offended on earth before she went after God."

"Did she take that well?" Mom asked.

Pettigrew smiled. "Not one bit. She got up and stomped out. Edith came back a week later. She had seen the light," the minister said. "I think she was trying to turn over a new leaf." I couldn't help thinking it was about time, but I kept my mouth closed.

There was no word when we would get Edith's body back from the Medical Examiner, so all the arrangements had to be tentative until we could set a date and a time. I went to the kitchen to help Scooter's mother and Graves followed me.

"Your family seems good about this," he said. "Are they as good as they seem?"

"I think so, they are a hardy group," I said, "but I'd keep them out of the house until they have it fully investigated and cleaned up. No open coffin."

Graves leaned near me. "I'm a member of the volunteer fire department and I heard about the hand," he whispered. "They'll hear nothing about the body from me." Undertakers aren't too high on my list of professions, but Graves was genuinely helpful. He knew the ropes and knew what to do to make things simpler.

Someone knocked on the door. It was a man named Byron Q. R. Sample who was Edith's lawyer. I noticed Elizabeth and Scooter were noticeably cooler to Byron than they were to Pettigrew and Graves. My mother noticed that too and the conversation became more restrained. Sample said she had a will, but it was in a constant state of flux, depending on whom she was feuding with at the time. She had a safety deposit box, and the will should be there.

Since Sample had power of attorney, he had access to the box. He offered to take Mom and my Aunts to the bank. They left with him in his big Mercedes. I left, so I could make some calls to my office. Scooter had to go and deal with the cows.

We were walking away from the house when it struck me. There were no State Troopers investigating the death. I asked Scooter about that.

"That's Willard Thompson's contribution to the problem. He has to call them in and he won't do it. As you saw, he thinks it's Mexicans," Scooter said. "He's really mad I called the Arson team. That's why he was so rude. Willard likes to solve problems himself, or sweep them under the table."

"This is a big problem to sweep away," I remarked.

"Willard's been here 40 years. He's lazy, but worse than that, he thinks he owns the town," Scooter explained.

"Boss Hogg style?"

"You got it. Most of the time crime here is open and shut. You know, a man kills his wife because she was messing around, hunting accidents, that sort of thing," Scooter continued. "This is different, but I'm sure Willard doesn't know it." Scooter went off to see his cows and I returned to the doublewide.

I called my office and all was well there. Richmond's criminal classes were taking a rare break. I told my right hand man, Frank, about the situation in Wythetown. He said he'd get our internet Geek squad looking around. We had a group of retirees who liked to do research on line. Several were retired policemen who still had connections in the force.

When I hung up, my cell phone rang immediately. It was Donnan. He wanted to chat. He asked if I could get by that evening at ten. "I don't want everyone to see who's coming and going," he explained.

"Do you want Scooter too?" I asked.

"He seems bright," Donnan said. "Is that the way you see it?"

"Unexpectedly professional," I replied. I then told him we would be there at 10:00. We had dinner at the house with Elizabeth and Scooter. It was a small town and neighbors had been dropping off food. After dinner, Scooter and I went into town.

We stopped at the Graves Funeral Home and spoke to Scooter's friend. Out of his undertaker's clothes, he was Billy, not William and he was a laid-back country boy. He lived in a converted garage behind the funeral home. It was his family's business, but his parents had moved into a modern house on the other side of town.

The garage was nice. We had a beer and chatted. Billy was up on all the gossip in town. Edith wasn't a popular woman, and a significant portion of the residents had threatened to kill her at one time or another. Her horrible death shocked everyone and Billy thought we'd have a good turnout at the funeral. "The combination of guilt and curiosity should give you a good crowd," Billy said. "That's the way it is here. By the way, the word is out that your Mom and Aunts are good people."

"Any word about me?" I asked.

"Too scrawny and ugly to get married, but a good son, is the way they see it," Billy said. Billy was on the beefy side and I had the feeling scrawny wasn't an asset in his mind.

"That's the way I like it," I said. "I like to fade into the woodwork." There was a little tension in the air. It took me a while to realize Scooter and Billy were playmates. It was a two's company, three's a crowd situation. I suggested I'd go on a walk to get the lay of the land. Poor Billy looked relieved. I left and said I'd be back in an hour.

Wythetown wasn't big and wasn't prosperous. There were two banks, several barbershops, a Sears catalog store and a few discount shops. The diner was the only business that was open. I went in and ordered a cup of coffee. I was the only customer. The waitress was an older woman who was tired and mean.

"Maybelle, why don't you go home? I'll take care of things," a big man yelled from the kitchen. "I'll close up too." The woman took off her apron, grabbed her purse and left.

A big, bearded man appeared at the kitchen door. "Sorry about Maybelle. One of the other waitresses didn't show," he said.

"I'll drink up fast and get out," I said.

"No need to do that. I'll give you another cup of coffee if you stay and talk to me as I clean up the counter," he said. "Andy Andraviranian is the name." We shook hands.

"Clydesdale Noland here," I said. "I'm here for a funeral. My Aunt burned up two days ago."

"Is that the poor woman on Elm Street?" he asked. I nodded. "Nasty business." We chatted for a while. Andy was a big man, wearing a white tee shirt. Tufts of hair made a fringe around his neck and he had arms that would make a gorilla proud. He had heard quite a bit about Edith's death, but not much of it was true. The local gossip was fast, but not very accurate.

I could see a young man walking by the dinner in the mirror behind the counter. He walked by several times. He seemed nervous and I was just about to get suspicious when he pulled on a mask and pulled out a gun. A second later he was in the diner, "Empty the cash register!" he demanded. "Hands up!"

Andy looked shocked and walked slowly toward the cash register. I just sat there. Apparently, the man didn't think I was worth worrying about. I was actually a little miffed. I'm small, but I'm not that small. The robber was shaking in a way I associated with drug problems. Andy opened the register and took the money out.

"Is that all?" the robber screamed. "I need more!" He cocked the pistol. I jumped him. He was totally surprised and I had the pistol out of his hand and in mine in a second. He was a big guy and I had to get him under my control before he recovered his senses enough to fight back.

I didn't need to worry. As soon as I got the gun, Andy beamed the guy with an iron frying pan. I heard a siren. Andy must have pushed a silent alarm.

"You're good at that," Andy said. "That scumbag had me worried." He looked at me closely. "That wasn't the first time you've done that was it?"

"I've had some law enforcement experience," I said. The police were here by now. The would-be robber was known to the troopers and they carried him off and said they'd get our statements the next day. They were gone in ten minutes.

"Very efficient," I said.

"I need a drink," Andy said. "Care to join me for a drink? I live upstairs." I said sure.

We went through the kitchen and up the stairs. The apartment was hot as hell. "Shit, I forgot to turn on the air conditioning!" Andy exclaimed. He flipped a switch. "It will be better in a minute," he added as he stripped off his shirt. "Let me get a clean shirt."

"No need on my account," I said. "You're in good shape. I don't mind." Andy went to the kitchenette and got drinks.

"I work out some," he said. "Working in a kitchen is filled with temptation. Everyone in my family tends to be heavy." Andy flexed his arms and then I felt his rock hard pecs.

"Nice and furry," I said as I tweaked his nipples. He sighed. A few seconds later, we were both naked on the floor going at it like dogs in heat.

At first I thought Andy had almost no cock. It was lost somewhere in the jungle of hair of his crotch. He turned out to be a grower, not a shower. Once he got excited, the cock turned into a solid six by six. When my finger strayed toward his ass hole, he began to leak. When I found his hole and pressed my finger into it, his cock exploded and I was drinking a week or two's supply of cum.

"Sorry about that," Andy said. "You got a big dose of Armenian high test." He looked at me. I smiled and he saw I still had some cum in my mouth. He kissed me and we shared his man seed. This got him going again and I felt cum splatter against my gut as he shot off again.

"We got to do this again," I said, "but I've got to get back to see a friend at ten."

"I owe you one," Andy said. "I don't usually shoot off so fast. I don't know what got into me."

"I'll just take that as a compliment," I said. "Maybe I'm not everyone's ideal of a dreamboat, but I do hit the spot sometimes."

"Are you gay?" Andy asked.

"I sure as hell am," I said and then I asked, "Are you?"

"I don't think so," Andy replied after a brief hesitation. "I like sex a lot, and I really enjoyed you." We said good-bye and I went to Graves' house. Scooter was waiting for me and we drove to Donnan's RV parked beside Aunt Edith's house.

Donnan was alone. The RV was dark with no lights on. "Come in guys," he said. "I need some back ground." Scooter repeated his narrative of the fire and added some information on possible suspects. They were few and far between. I gave him a quick biography of Aunt Edith. I went through her attraction to radical "Christian" groups.

"Did she have money?" Donnan asked.

"Not money with a capital M, but she was well off. Her husband did well in business and I don't think they spent a penny," I said. "My Mom and Aunts went to the bank this afternoon, but they didn't say anything."

"They found nothing exceptional?" Donnan asked.

"I'll ask. Mom and her sisters don't talk about money."

"A sign of bad breeding?" Donnan suggested.

Scooter laughed. "Just like my Mom," he said. "She'd never talk about money outside the family. It was the sort of thing you might whisper about after the kids were in bed, but never in public."

Donnan said it was Arson, as we knew and very crude Arson. "There's nothing professional about the event," he said. "It was crudely done and ineffectual. It made a mess rather than real damage. I sent my field man back to Roanoke to get things tested. It's just a formality, it's open and shut."

We talked for a while. Scooter had to take a piss, and I was alone with Donnan. "Are you the Clydesdale who's a good friend of Fire Hose?" he whispered. Fire Hose was a well-hung friend of mine in Richmond, Vince DeSoto. His nickname described his cock.

"As a matter of fact I am," I said. "He's an old and playful friend."

"I'd like to . . . let's say get to know you better," Donnan whispered. He was glancing at the toilet room door down the hall of the RV.

"Scooter's a member of the Fraternity," I said. "He's okay. Are you offended by a threesome?"

"Shit no," he replied instantly. "There's a cot in the back room."

Donnan was a sucker. That was good for me since Andy had revved me up and I was ready for more fun. When Scooter got out of the toilet, he called, "Where are you guys?" I called to him and said we were relaxing. He joined us.

Donnan was a big man and more than a bit over weight. He didn't want to undress. I told him I liked my sex naked. It was dark, so he did it. I was sitting on the cot as he sucked me. Scooter got behind him and rubbed his cock in Donnan's ass crack. Donnan didn't object. He couldn't get much of my cock into his mouth, but he enjoyed it as it grew. He liked size and I had what he wanted.

Scooter was rimming him now and spitting into the hole. Donnan adjusted his position, so Scooter would have better access. I've never thought spit was a particularly good lubricant, but I seemed to work for Scooter and more importantly for Donnan. He shivered when the head cleared the sphincter, but just moaned and twitched as Scooter cock probed deeply into his ass.

Once Scooter was fully lodged, Donnan resumed his sucking activities. Scooter started slowly, and then built up speed. He suddenly slowed down.

"I can go fast if you want to give Clydesdale a try, or I can slow down and take my time?" Scooter asked. "What's your poison?"

"I wouldn't mind trying Clydesdale's cock," Donnan whispered. However, before we could change positions, Scooter cried out. "There's someone in the house!"

He was standing and could see out the window of the RV. Wythetown seemed to be filled with potential playmates, but somehow my balls were still filled and needed draining. We got dressed and went after the prowler.

Part 3

Donnan was a good man but he wasn't built for speed or stealth. I'm afraid a herd of Buffalos had a better chance of a sneak attack. After searching fruitlessly for the prowler, we returned to the RV and called the cops and Donnan called in reinforcements.

"It could be a looter, but it could be someone who had left something, or wanted to find something in the house," Donnan said. "We need to do a fine tooth comb search." He also called in the State Police.

"You'll piss off Chief Thompson," Scooter said.

"I'm not too worried about that," Donnan said. "He hasn't exactly been helpful. The whole situation smells bad. There's trouble in River City and it ain't pool."

I offered to stay and watch for the rest of the night, but Donnan said he'd do that. "I'm wide awake now."

Scooter and I returned to the farm. I was bushed and went right to bed. I hate to sleep with a full load still brewing in my balls, but it happens sometimes. The next morning I asked my Mom what the found in the lock box at the bank.

Mom hesitated. "Come on Mom. Someone murdered her. There may be a clue in the box."

"Clydesdale is right," Aunt Ellen said. "It was a big box and filled to the brim. We didn't find the will, but there were deeds, stock certificates and certificates of deposit."

"No will you said?" I asked.

"No will." Mom replied. I went to the phone and called Donnan. I told him the will was missing and might be somewhere in the house.

"The big crime scene unit from Roanoke will be here at noon," Donnan said. "If it's in the house, they'll find it." I returned to the kitchen table.

"Mr. Sample said the properties didn't have any value," Ellen said.

"I might like a second opinion on that," Elizabeth said. "Byron Sample isn't crooked, but he has been known to stray near the edge once and a while. Did he offer to take the properties off your hands?"

"How did you know that?" Mom asked. Elizabeth gave a knowing smile.

"Let's just say, his offers reflect the assessed valuation rather than the market value," Elizabeth said. "When my husband died, he offered me $150,000.00 for the farm. Scooter was insulted."

"How can we get a realistic valuation?" Aunt Sarah asked,

"I know a retired real estate man," Elizabeth said. "He's an old friend and a card-carrying member of the Courthouse gang. He'll know."

"Did you ask about the checking account?" I asked.

"Darn, we forgot," Mom said. "Maybe we can do that today. We do have to pay for the funeral expenses and cleaning up the house. When can we go to the house?"

"Not now," I replied. I told them about the events of the last night and they understood.

"Edith had some of Momma's things," Ellen said. "Can you ask them to be careful? Edith got a majority of the things in the house when Momma died. She wasn't married at the time and didn't have anything. Did you see the big green soup tureen?"

"No, I didn't but everything was sooty," I replied.

"Our mother used to put important things in the tureen," Ellen said. "If there are important papers in the house, that's where Edith might put something like a will."

"Well, Donnan said they were going to use a fine tooth comb. I take that to mean they're going to be careful and look at everything."

I wanted to go into town and see what was up. My Mom and Aunts needed the Buick, but Elizabeth offered the use of the jalopy. It was the car Scooter had as teenager. "It still runs well, but it not an impressive vehicle," she said.

The jalopy was an old, slightly souped-up Dodge Dart. There were NASCAR stickers on the worst rust spots. It was perfect. I felt 18 again. I went into town. I stopped first at the funeral home to see if there was any word on the body. Billy had called the Medical Examiner. They thought the body would be released that afternoon.

"If it's of any comfort, she was dead well before the mutilation and the fire," Billy said. "A single blow to the head killed her. She died instantly."

It was odd, but I did feel better. "Scooter told me you are a big boy," Billy whispered.

"Are you into size?"

"No," Billy said decisively. "Well, maybe a little." He looked at me sheepishly. "You may think you've run into a bunch of fags, but we aren't gay. We just mess around some."

I looked him in the eye. "I am gay and I mess around lots." The doorbell rang and some customers came in, so I left. I went to the diner. It was closed. I went to the back and found a doorbell next to a rear entrance. After pressing it, Andy appeared.

He looked mad until he saw me, then he smiled.

"Closed because of the robbery?"

"Hell no! This is my fishing day," Andy answered. "This is a small town and they understand that. Come on in."

We went upstairs and he gave me a cup of coffee. "Is sex with you always that good?" he asked. "I'd forgotten what it was like. I'm not much of a lady's man."

"Sex with me depends what you're into," I answered. "If you like your men manly and don't mind if they're short, I'm the guy for you."

"Short and hung like King Kong?"

"You noticed?"

Andy laughed. "I sure did. It looks like something you would find preserved in a bottle at the Smithsonian. It's huge. Would you mind if we did it again?"

"Well, I'm fully loaded and cocked," I said. "Do you think you could suck me until I shoot?"

Andy looked uncertain. "I can try."

"Do you like to get fucked?" I asked. Now Andy looked really uncertain. I continued talking, "Hey Andy. I drained the sperm from your entire reproductive system last night. I'm not the shy type and whatever you like or don't like is fine with me." I was getting undressed as we chatted. I figured that would keep Andy interested.

"Well, I've done a little experimenting," Andy admitted. "Not with guys, but experimenting."

"Dildos?"

"Sort of," Andy said, "I've used what's available." Andy was naked now and really excited. I couldn't figure out what Andy was talking about and then I realized he was a cook. I guessed a carrot or zucchini would meet his needs.

"Was your experimenting successful?" I asked. He blushed and then nodded. "Have you worked up to something big, like a zucchini?" He blushed again. I had guessed right.

"I did a cucumber," he admitted.

"How was it?"

"Good," he said. "I liked it."

"Never had a cock in your ass, though?"

"No, I was too embarrassed," he said. "I don't know anyone who would do it with me. It's a small town."

I was hard as a rock now. Andy was staring at my engorged cock. "Do you think you'd like to try the real thing?"

"Can you take it slow?" he asked. I took that as a yes.

"You just relax and leave yourself in Dr. Clydesdale's hands," I said. "I want you to enjoy this as much as I do. I've done this before and I know what I'm doing."

"Do you get many repeat customers?"

"I sure do," I replied. "I'm still getting Christmas card from a guy I fucked once in 1983."

Andy laughed. "Maybe I'll take just half?"

It was my turn to laugh. "You just want to get half fucked? Do you have some lubricant?"

"Extra virgin olive oil," he said. "I'm a cook. It's always available."

"I need to open you up some," I said. "Do you have something I could work in your hole? I've never used a vegetable as a dildo before. It kind of turns me on." Andy got the olive oil while I checked out his vegetable drawer. I picked out a large and long carrot and a beefy zucchini. The carrot had been cleaned and I suspected Andy might have had other plans for it.

I'm not usually much of an asshole man, but when I got Andy on his back with his legs spread and his hole exposed, I liked what I saw. He had swirls of hair covering, muscular buns. In the center was the pink pillow of the sphincter muscle with a delicate rosebud in the middle. It was pretty.

I put some oil on my finger and played with the rosebud. Andy twitched when the cool oil touched his ass. I planned to finger fuck him and then use the vegetables. For a grand finale, I would fuck him to the moon and back. Somehow, my tongue made the first attack on his ass.

Neither Andy nor I expected that. His ass was tight, but eventually he relaxed enough for me to get my tongue past the sphincter a little. He was moaning and begged me to get something deeper into his ass. I got the carrot, coated it in oil and eased it through the pucker. Damn if I didn't get my tongue back in his hole, pushing the carrot deeper.

I pushed his legs back and as his body reacted normally, trying to expel the foreign object from his ass, I started to nibble on it. I'm not into shit, but Andy was clean as a whistle. I ended up munching on it. Andy was going crazy.

There was a zucchini waiting, but I couldn't wait. It was time for the main attraction. "I can't wait any longer. I've got to get in your ass," I said. "Are you ready?"

"Shit yes!" Andy exclaimed.

I stood up and coated my cock with the oil. I pulled him to the edge of the bed and the pushed his legs back so they were against his chest. His ass was wide open and defenseless. While he looked a little worried, he looked more excited. While I had been working on his ass, he had been leaking pre cum. His gut was covered in the stuff. I collected some on my hand and added it to the oil on my cock. Natural lube is the best and he was oozing buckets of it. You don't often get to fuck a guy using his own precum as lube. It was a nice touch.

I nosed my cock head into his quivering hole. I told myself to slow down and take my time. I bounced my cock head against his pucker. With each little bounce, I got a little deeper. "Relax and let me in," I whispered. I remembered when I had touched his tits the night before he got excited. I reached over and pinched each tit gently.

Andy's tits were like an automatic garage door opener. As I pinched, his ass lost its muscle tone and my cock slipped slowly into his ass. I didn't shove it; I just eased forward until every inch was in his rectum. Andy moaned and his eyes rolled back into his head. It was beautiful.

I let go of his tits and his ass contracted, grabbing my cock with his ass muscles. I thrust a little. He had a sphincter or iron. It was a natural cock ring, keeping me rock hard. Then I tweaked his tits and he opened wide.

The next fifteen minutes were great. It was good for me, but it was phenomenal for Andy. I knew he had discovered parts of his body he didn't know existed and he was feeling all new sensations. It was a battle for me not to shoot off. He had the ass of my dreams. Andy began to shoot. When he did, his ass convulsed. That was enough to push me over the edge. My cock shot the ripe cum in my balls into the deepest recess of his body.

"What in hell happened?" Andy asked once he got his breath back.

"I hate to break it to you, but you aren't a virgin anymore," I said. "And unless I have badly misjudged what just happened, you're also a man who's seriously into his ass. You liked what just happened?"

"Damn, I didn't know you could feel so much," he said. "I got dizzy it was so good. I had no idea"

"I have to get over to the house, but I sure want to do this again." I said as I got up.

"Is it always this good?" Andy asked.

"For you it will be," I said. "You're a natural bottom. There is nothing but good spots in your ass." Andy was still on the bed. I leaned over, quickly worked my finger into his ass and pressed his prostate. Andy moaned.

"Damn, that's good," Andy cried. "But not as good as the cock."

"I have to go, but I'll be back," I said. I washed up, got dressed and left.

I got to Aunt Edna's house five minutes later. There was another RV on the street. This was a State Police crime scene unit. Donnan was talking with a trooper. I went over.

"Trooper Morris. This is Clydesdale Noland," Donnan said in introduction. "He's the nephew of the victim." We shook hands.

"My Aunts said to look in the soup tureen for the will," I said. "It's a traditional family hiding place."

"Trooper Smith," Morris bellowed. "Look for a soup tureen."

"What in hell is a tureen?" Smith yelled back.

"Watch the fucking Food Channel! Get some culture!" Morris replied. "It's a large covered bowl for soup. Usually there's a place for the ladle. Don't ask me what a ladle is!"

"There are some antiques and heirlooms there. My Aunts are worried they might get broken. They're not valuable, just important to my Aunts," I said. Donnan burst out in laughter.

"Clydesdale, Trooper Morris is called Bull by those who know him. He's a regular Bull in a china shop," Donnan explained.

A Buick appeared on the street. It stopped and my mother and two Aunts got out and came over to us.

"Clydesdale, I remembered something. I though you should know." Mom said. I introduced her to Donnan and Morris. "When we were girls, we had a secret hiding place under the bottom step of the attic stair. Edith always hid her most secret things there. You might look there."

"Thank you Ma'am," Morris said. He went into the house.

"We went to the bank. Her checking account was much depleted," Ellen said. "A series of four and five hundred dollar checks made out to cash. They were all within the last six months."

"Is there an obvious explanation?" Donnan asked.

"Very odd," Ellen said. "Edith was a skinflint. When we went on little vacation, she would cash a check for twenty and expect it to last a week."

"It sounds like blackmail," I said.

"That would be hard to believe," Sarah said. "Her life was blameless, except for the lack of charity and kindness to others, of course."

"It might be one of her fire and brimstone charities," Mom suggested. "Just give us the money in cash. We can get it right to the need that way. Edith would fall for that line. She distrusted everyone except religious con men."

"Give that lady a gold ring!" Morris bellowed from an upstairs window. "I found the will. I found two wills." Morris was with us a minute later with two envelops. Trooper Smith emerged from the house with a large, soot-covered tureen at the same time. We took them into the Police RV.

The tureen contained some antique jewelry, and a ledger book. There was also something that looked like a deed. There was one will was dated six months earlier, the other was two weeks old. Trooper Morris was a stickler for procedure and he wanted recorded and professionally examined before they were examined. It was disappointing, but I understood his reasoning. The police wanted to know what was in the will and other information before it became general information.

My Mom and Aunts were probably heirs, and thus possible suspects. I explained this to my Mom. She was actually flattered that anyone could consider that option. "I've never been a dangerous woman before," she said. They had an appointment with Billy Graves to make final arrangements for the funeral. They heard the body was on its way.

One of the Policemen told me to go to the Station to give my statement on the attempted robbery of the dinner. That took all afternoon. Wythetown's Police Department didn't have two crimes at the same time. Their resources were stretched thin.

Part 4

I had a long talk with Chief Thompson while I was there. He seemed to have mellowed. I hadn't thought he was the kind of man who would apologize and rethink his approach. I was wrong. He saw the writing on the wall and realized his Mexican theory wasn't going to fly. He bragged to me about how good his department was and I realized if the State Police were involved, he needed to show some signs of efficiency. He had genuine pride in his department.

He had made calls and found out about Clydesdale & Company and now knew my reputation. "If we can be of help to you, just let me know," he said. "I'd appreciate it if you can help me when you can. I don't like what's going on here. It's not the usual."

"You're as well connected as anyone in these parts," I said. "What do the jungle drums say?"

"That's what is worrying me," the Chief said. "There is not a peep. It's like a lightning bolt out of the blue. That why I was pushing the Mexicans. They have their own community."

"Are there any strangers in the area?"

"No one I've noticed, but I'm checking on that," he said. "The only motel here isn't really fit for humans, but I'm checking in Martinsville and Bristol."

"Is it possible you just don't want a local involved?"

"Of course I don't want a local involved, but there's some logic behind my thinking," he explained. "We're a small town and I know just about everybody here. I know their parents and grandparents too. There is nothing to suggest this sort of thing would happen. I have a good idea who thinking about screwing his daughter and who dreams about fucking a minor. I know who's interested in fires and who gets violent when they get shit-faced drunk."

"Your Aunt was an irritating woman. She rubbed me the wrong way most of the time, but it was irritation, not rage she inspired. Beating an elderly woman to death and chopping up her body is not on the radar screen," he said. "If there was anyone who had any tendencies that way, they'd be in jail by now." I'm usually skeptical about locals who think it must be a stranger, but Thompson seemed to know his stuff.

I went to give my statement to the officer handling the diner robbery. Officer Sue Belmont was young and a bit officious, but once we got into the statement she relaxed. She was new to the force and this was her biggest case to date. I thought she would become a good police office when she had more experience.

When I finished the statement Rollie saw me and gave me a tour of the offices. It was after six, the day crew had left, and the evening watch was already on patrol. The Police Department was fueled by strong coffee. Since I was stuck there for most of the afternoon, I had drunk at least three and maybe four cups of coffee. I have a bladder the size of a small New England state, but when we hit the basement locker room, I took a leak. Someone was taking a shower in the next room.

I was pissing when a naked man left the shower room and stood at the urinal next to me. It was the chief. Thompson was one of the rare older men who look better naked than dressed. He wasn't Charles Atlas, but he obviously worked out and spent a lot of time outdoors. He had a good tan.

With a dusting of blond mixed with white hair on his chest, I suspected he had shaved it recently. His hairy ball sack held two apricot-sized balls. As far as I could tell, his cock consisted only of a cut, flared, cock head the size of a silver dollar. He certainly didn't mind being naked in front of a stranger.

"I like your high test coffee, but it has a side effect," I said.

"I figure either the caffeine, or the need to take a leak will keep you awake, one way, or the other," he said.

"It seems to me it's a 50/50 proposition," I commented. "This is fancy locker area. I've not seen many like it."

"You are in the emergency command center for the county, paid for by the Feds and the Commonwealth," he explained. "We got it after hurricane Camille. We have back up power for three weeks." He leaned close to me, "How long does it take for the piss to get from your bladder to the end of your dick? You got a long one."

"In no time at all," I replied. "It's an expressway."

The Chief laughed. "I've got a shack a few miles from here. Why don't you come over for some burgers? I wouldn't mind an off the record chat with you."

"I guess I could do that," I said. "Where is it?"

"Rollie's coming. He'll give you a ride," Thompson said. "He's going to get Scooter to come. I've got some fences to mend with Scooter."

I finished the tour with Rollie, called Mom, and told her I was going to dinner with the Chief. They were going to dinner with one of Elizabeth's friends. "It's going to be 100% old lady talk," she said. "You'd be bored to tears."

"Keep your ears open," I said. "Old ladies hear things too." Mom and her sisters were intelligent women. Ellen was a murder mystery fan, so I knew she would be alert.

Rollie had changed into civilian clothes and we drove into the countryside. Wythetown is in the boonies, but the countryside outside of Wythetown was dismal. Coal mining doesn't enhance the landscape any way, but the land was dreary. We turned off the road and drove down a rutted trail and then into a heavily wooded area. There must not have been coal under this patch.

Chief Thompson's shack was just that. It was covered in asphalt shingles and looked like crap. Inside it was a little bit better, but not a lot. It was one room with a kitchen area to one end and a sleeping loft. There was a bath attached to the side. The windows on the back overlooked a really pretty pond.

"Welcome to the ugliest shack in the Blue Ridge," Thompson said as he greeted us. "My wife and daughters hate it, so it's just perfect for me. This is a man's place."

We walked out to the back porch and looked at the view. It was beautiful, with the blue sky reflected in the clear water of the pond. "How did this escape the coal company?" I asked.

"This is the General Manager's fishing place," Thompson explained. I sat on an old wicker chair next to a hammock. It was oddly supported and small.

"Is that what I think it is?" I asked looking at the hammock.

Thompson smiled. "It's my own invention. Rollie's my nephew and I found out about his sexual tastes years ago. He loves the sling," the Police Chief said. "His birthday's coming up so we were going to have a little celebration here, just four or five men. Rollie said he thought you'd be interested. If you're not, you don't need to stay. I hope you're not offended by group sex?"

"You think I'm the kind of guy who will have sex with any Tom Dick and Harry who comes along?" I said sternly. The chief looked taken aback. "Well if you think that, you'd be exactly right! What are the guys like?"

He smiled. "Damn, you had me going there for a minute," Thompson said. "Rollie's usually quite good about that sort of thing. He's a good judge of character. Rollie has the best gaydar of any man I've ever met."

I was hoping to get a preview of coming attractions, but someone drove up. Two older men got out, one white, one black. It took me a second to realize one was Rev. Pettigrew. The Chief introduced the other as Coach Brown. A State Police cruiser arrived next. I hadn't expected to see Troopers Morris and Smith again.

There was a slightly uncomfortable period as we chatted on the porch. Everyone knew why we were here, but not how to get the ball rolling. Rollie solved the problem. He emerged from the front door naked and semi erect.

"Damn, Uncle Willard," he said. "Am I the only bottom here?"

"It's your birthday, I thought I give you a real workout," the Chief said. "Is that a problem?"

"Hell no. When do we get started?" Rollie asked. "Who's first?"

"There's one special thing I'd like for you guys to do," the Chief said. "Rollie told me he'd like to take a load from each of you. He wants the cream. It's his birthday and that seems fair enough. It might get a bit messy later on, so any of you who are worried about the mess, get first in line."

"I've got no problem with sloppy seconds," Rev. Pettigrew said, "I'll go to the end of the line, if you don't mind."

It turned out no one seemed to be squeamish. We went into the house, stripped naked and then went to the rear porch. Rollie was in the sling with his legs spread wide and his ass open.

"We need a fluffer," Trooper Morris said. "Trooper Smith, are you up for it?"

"Yes Sir!" he replied with a military salute. He pumped iron and had a crew cut. Rev. Pettigrew was first in line. I think Smith was a good-looking man and Pettigrew wanted him fresh. Smith dropped to his knees and swallowed the preacher's cock whole.

When I looked over the assembled men, I marveled at the variety available in men's external genitalia. We all had balls, sack, shaft and head, but some balls were nuts, others are fruits; some sacks hang low and other are held tight against the body. There were beer can shafts and mosquito dicks. Thompson had a mushroom head. Smith had a bullet gland. I admit to having my preferences, but in all my years messing around with men, I've discovered you can never tell which cock will do the trick.

While Smith sucked the Preacher, Coach Brown was to first to pop Rollie's cherry. You could tell Brown had been muscular, but he must have been in his upper sixties now and had somewhat gone to pot. He cock was a thick, uncut, seven-inch specimen. He coated it with lubricant and rammed it in deep on the first thrust. It wasn't an elegant fuck, but Rollie took it well. He was winded at first, but then began to whimper.

Rollie was hairy, but his skin was pale white. Coach Brown's cock was coal black except for his cock head. It was a purplish lavender color. Watching the black cock plunge into Rollie's pink ass was a sight. The audience got turned on.

"How long have you been fucking this pup?" Morris asked Coach Brown.

"Rollie and I go way back," Brown said. "Willard found out about Rollie's interests and asked if I would be the first to pop his cherry. He knew about my fucking technique and figured I might cure the boy of his interests. Damn if Rollie didn't love it!"

"The best made plans . . ."

"Damn, I'm shooting!" Brown exclaimed. He rammed Rollie with great vigor six or seven times, then pulled out suddenly, his cock was still ejaculating. Several volleys coated Rollie's hole and the rest splattered against Rollie's balls. Rev. Pettigrew was next in line. He was hard now. His cock was thin and long. He didn't fuck. He caressed the insides of Rollie's ass with his organ. Rollie's ass was glistening with cum and lubricant. Pettigrew played with Rollie's tits and Rollie reached up and tweaked the Preacher's nipples. Pettigrew shot off immediately.

I was watching the sling when Morris came up to me and started sucking. Somehow, I thought he was more to the aggressive top type, but from the way he sucked my member, it was clear he was a cock man. Thompson was in his nephew's ass now, but it was hard to watch, since I was preoccupied by Morris's expert cock sucking. I was getting close, so when the Chief pulled out, I stepped up to the sling.

Rollie looked a bit worn and frazzled by now. I was the fourth guy in his ass so he was tired. His cock was a bit limp now, but when my cock head cleared his sphincter, he revived. His cock perked up too. His sphincter had neither lost its muscle tone, nor was just plain worn out. He couldn't fight me, but it was a nice, snug fit. I took my time.

I've never liked dry fucking and I like lube. There's something about homemade man lube that really hits the spot for me. I like cornhuskers and Wet, but sperm is the best. I'm not sure I can feel the difference, but knowing millions of little sperms are easing my way give me a rush. Someone told me there could easily be 40 to 50 million sperms in an orgasm. With Coach, the preacher and Thompson's cream, they most have been a good 200 million little pollywogs easing my way in to Rollie's ass. It was good.

It was a nice, laid-back group of men. Scooter and Willy Graves had appeared as well as a man I didn't know. Most guys were stoking or sucking, but when I started to fuck, they clustered around the sling to watch.

"Damn, I don't believe that fuck tool fits!" Smith said. "It would split me in half." I'm not an exhibitionist, but I don't mind being admired. I looked over to Smith and our eyes met. I wasn't too sure I'd split him in half and had a strong premonition my cock head would get intimate with his prostate before the night was over. My cock pushed the hair around Rollie's ass onto his hole. When I pulled out the hair and some of Rollie's insides came out, all coated in sperm.

It was getting messy. Most gay porn features well-groomed men who never break into a sweat and never need to comb their hair. A cock wedged between shaved balls and neatly trimmed pubes slides into a shaved asshole. Once and a while the fucker gets excited. Most of the time the bottom could be getting a manicure for all the excitement he shows.

I'd bet porn stars like sex as much as I do, but they can't show it. Rollie and I were into it and everyone knew. I didn't last as long as I'd have liked too, but the excitement got to me and I shot off. I'm not a verbal person when it comes to sex. However, damn if I didn't growl, then roar when I rear loaded Rollie. Everybody knew what I was doing. They applauded. I should have been embarrassed, but you can't be embarrassed during an orgasm.

I pulled out. Scooter took my place. His cock must have been refreshing after my ass stretcher. I sat down on a chair and cooled off. The remains of my orgasm drooled from my cock. I was talking with Coach Brown when Morris crawled over and began to lick of my cock drool. He apparently liked the sperm concoction coating my cock.

When Trooper Morris was finished, Brown and I went to the pond and took a swim. It was a warm day and the water was crystal clear. After fifteen minutes, the rest of the men joined us, including Rollie. He had taken the last load from the last man. Rollie was tired looking, but he had a blissful look to him. I think the evening was a success.

Chief Thompson had a dinner of fried chicken and slaw, all provided by KFC. It wasn't fancy, but it hit the spot. It began to get dark. I don't know why, but darkness seems to bring out the lustiness in most men. Everyone had shot off before dinner, but I still had one or two orgasms in me. I wasn't the only one.

Trooper Smith stayed close to me. Smith's real name was Oliver, but they called him Boomer. Boomer had a strong accent and only modest grip on English Grammar. As I talked to him, I realized he was smart enough, but poorly educated and had very little knowledge of the world. I felt sympathy for him, since I'd been in a similar situation when I was younger.

Boomer said his Daddy was dumb as shit and damn proud of it. He looked up to Trooper Morris as a god. No one had ever taken any interest in him before. "Morris is bossy, but if I do exactly what he says, it just turns out right," Boomer said.

Another guy stayed near me. This was the man who had arrived late with Scooter and Billy. He tended to stare at my cock. He was of middle height and had a full beard. While he had a muscular upper body, he had a deformed leg and walked with a bad limp. He didn't say anything and I didn't know what to think about him when Scooter came to me and introduced the man.

"Clydesdale, this is Festus. He's a nice guy," I shook hands. Scooter whispered in my ear. "He's a good kid, but handicapped. He's almost deaf and it takes some time explaining what he needs to do. Once he gets it, all is well. Mom thinks if they had sent him to the right schools, he'd be fine. Festus is the dishwasher at the diner."

"You work for Andy?" I asked.

Festus' face broke into a smile. "Andy's my boss. He's a good man." I put my arm around him. He snuggled closer and started playing with the hair on my chest. "George of the Jungle," he muttered.

Scooter laughed. "He seems to think you're a monkey."

"Well, I guess that's better than being called that fucking Chimpanzee," I said. "That phrase pops up from time to time."

Scooter whispered to me again, "Festus likes sex. Don't worry about him. He's more than okay with it."

As his hands explored my body, they reached my cock. He played with it for a little and then looked up at me. "King Kong?" he said. We all burst out laughing. Festus was pleased. "Can I suck it?" he asked.

"Be my guest." I said. Boomer looked disappointed, so I pulled him close and began to fondle his cock. Festus was an equal opportunity sucker and when Boomer's cock came in range, he sucked it too. Festus had a wide mouth and he could get both in.

Eventually the three of us got on the grass and formed a small daisy chain. Boomer felt better when he got to suck my cock. I was sucking Festus, so Festus was sucking Boomer. Festus' cock was a solid, uncut, six-inch cock with a big mushroom head. He had huge balls that produced pre cum in generous amounts. It was tasty and exciting.

We traded places and I sucked Boomer. He had no pre cum until I worked my finger into his ass. When I pressed his prostate, I opened the pre cum floodgates. The light was dim now, but Festus saw me fingering Boomer's ass. I guessed Boomer wanted to try my cock, but I wasn't sure how to bring the subject up. I went off to get a coke and when I came back, Boomer was on his hands and knees taking Festus' cock doggy style.

Festus looked at me, winked and a second or two later, he pulled his cock out and shoved mine in. Boomer almost passed out from the shock, but when he recovered he loved it. I saw Morris looked at him twitching on my cock with satisfaction. Somehow, he reminded me of a mother bird who was watching her chick fly for the first time. Boomer shot off and fell asleep on the grass.

Chief Thompson came over to us and fucked Festus for a while. It was odd; he just came up to Festus and made him get on his hands and knees. Thompson worked his cock into Festus' hole without a word being said. He and Festus were smiling, so this was apparently, what they did.

I went wandering off and found Scooter taking Billy's cock. Billy has a wide stance so his ass was wide open. I poked my cock at the open hole and damn if he didn't open wide and let me in. Billy's chute was well lubricated and smooth as silk. After a while, Scooter wiggled out from under us and popped his thin probe into my ass. That was really satisfactory.

Later I fucked Scooter while Billy fucked me. I hadn't done a round robin like this in years. All of us were satisfied.

Part 5

I slept well that night and woke ready to do some real investigating. Unfortunately, there was Aunt Edith. Her body had returned and there was to be something at the funeral home that evening. The funeral was to be the next day. I must have looked unhappy about that. Mom told me to get into town and see how the investigation was going.

"Nothing could make me feel better than to have Edith's killer under arrest," she said. I went into town in the jalopy and had breakfast at the diner. Andy was cooking and Festus was washing dishes. I talked with the men at the counter. The men were mostly talking about the murder.

"She was a bitch, but I never thought anything like his might happen," one man said. He was called Slim. It was a joke name since he was anything but Slim.

"The Chief seems to think it was Mexicans," another man, named Hal, said.

"I don't like the Mexicans, but I don't think it was them. She never got within miles of a Mexican," Slim said. "She liked the Holy Rollers. My Old Lady use to go to the same church."

"The True Believers?" Hal asked. Slim nodded. "She must have liked it when the Preacher took off with Bessie Grant."

Slim chuckled. "She thought the Preacher was pure and chaste. It turned out he was only pure when it came to dried-up old hags," Slim said. "The old ladies were good for the collection plate and nothing else. I think Edith paid for the fucker's trip to Reno."

"The last time I saw Edith was at the True Value. She was with a young guy, a surveyor type, buying some tools," Hal said.

"She snagged herself a young one?" Slim suggested.

"It looked all business to me. They went off in his truck, Capitol Exploration, it said," Hal continued. "I have no idea what she was up to." The two men left making lewd comments about Edith and the young man. Festus saw me and came out to say hello. Andy was surprised and wanted to know how we met. I told him it was a long story.

I called my office on the cell phone and asked them to do some research on Capitol Exploration and then I went to Edith's house. Donnan saw me and asked me in. "The wills are interesting," he said. "The older will leave everything except for some heirlooms to some odd church, the True Bible Church, or something like that."

"The True Believers?" I suggested. Donnan looked at me for a minute.

"You do get around, don't you?" he remarked. "The other leaves it all to the local library and to your Mother and Aunts. There's a paragraph asking forgiveness for being so pompous. Was she that bad?"

"I'm afraid she was," I said. "She had a knack of draining the enjoyment from every holiday dinner I ever went to. What were the other papers?"

"There's a deed to the Old Blue Mining company property, the deed to the house and some stock certificates," he said. "It seems her husband owned the mineral rights to most of the local mines. Worthless, I'll bet, but we'll check into it."

I went into the house and saw Trooper Smith carefully going through each of the items in the breakfront. "Is this the stuff your Mom's worried about?" he asked.

"That's it," I said. "It belonged to her Mama. Have you found anything?"

"Just this," he said. He produced a safe deposit box key. It said Box 412, Central Southside Virginia Bank.

"Rollie says that bank was bought out years ago," Smith said. "The building is still on Main Street."

I walked around the house. There were several officers sifting through the ashes and debris. "Oh Jesus," a female officer cried out. "I found an ear." I felt sick again. I decided to leave.

I got in the car and my cell phone rang. It was Frank, my office manager. "The geek squad hit pay dirt. Capitol Exploration looks for oil and natural gas," he said. "On the surface they look like a small time outfit, but they have the big boys behind them. They're a front for Metropolis-Occidental Petroleum."

"They are big boys," I said. "Keep on looking and let me know what shows up."

"Will do," Frank replied.

I went to the Police Station and asked about the Central Southside Bank. I told Thompson about the key. "Is there any chance anything is left in the building?" I asked.

"I doubt it, but it might be worth a visit. I was bought out by the CFB, which in turn was bought by the Fed Banc, than then by Wachovia. It closed really suddenly and they may have left something behind. I'll get a court order. I try and get it done today."

I saw my Mom drive by, so I got in my car and followed her. She stopped at St. John's Episcopal Church. She was glad to see me, her sister's were at the funeral home and she was to complete arranging the service and had to find the burial plot. That should have been easy, but Edith had four deeds to cemetery plots. Her husband had died midwinter in a blizzard and no one had been able to get to the funeral. No one knew where he was buried, so Mom and Rev. Pettigrew were going to look for it.

Pettigrew and another man were waiting for us. The man was the organist, Tom Robinson, and wanted to know some of Edith's favorite hymns. Mom knew them all, so she gave the man the information and left with Pettigrew. Tom offered to show me the church. I wasn't interested, but said yes to be polite.

The church was pretty and very fancy. The mine owners' went to this church, so they had Tiffany windows and all the fittings of a wealthy Episcopalian church. Tom explained this to me as we looked around. "Fortunately, they also endowed the church, which is why they have a full time organist," he said. Tom was my height, but weighed 40 or 50 pounds more than me. It was odd to be with a man I could look in the eye.

"Rollie's an old friend of mine," Tom said. "I was sorry not to be able to make it to the party last night. Father John said a good time was had by all. Rollie is a member of the choir here."

"Rollie seems to have gotten around," I remarked. I was ready for Tom to make a pass at me when a man entered the church.

"Sorry to interrupt you, but I got a call from Father John about a funeral. The message was garbled. What day is it and what time?" he asked.

"Tomorrow at 11:00," Tom said. "Jonathan, this is Mr. Noland. He's the nephew of the deceased. Mr. Noland, this is Jonathan Elliot, the County Clerk." We shook hands. Jonathan didn't strike me as a leader of men.

"Sorry for your loss," Jonathan said. "I assist at funerals. Rev. Mr. Pettigrew is good about that sort of event. He gives a very comforting service. Your Aunt was a well-known woman. Her husband left her well provided for."

"I never thought of her as wealthy," I said. "She didn't spend anything as far as I knew."

"She was frugal. Her husband bought many of the properties when the mines went belly up." Jonathan said. "He acquired the mineral rights to the ones he didn't buy outright. They were considered worthless at the time, but he felt you could never know the future."

"Has there been any interest in the properties recently?"

"As a matter of fact there has been some recently," Jonathan replied. "Several parties have been doing research in the last six months."

"Who were they?"

"They were very private persons," Jonathan replied. "In my experience, persons doing early research in real estate tend to be closed mouthed. Discretion is important. You might mention this conversation to the heirs. I would be careful of a quick sale."

"We've met Mr. Sample," I said. Jonathan smiled.

"Clydesdale went to the little party for Rollie last night," Tom mentioned casually. "John said he acquitted himself well, very well."

"A Board of Supervisors' meeting last night occupied my time," Jonathan said. "Rollie's not exactly my type, but a good boy."

"What is your type?" I asked.

"Jonathan likes them young and pretty," Tom said. "But he seems to put up with others well."

"Just because I like caviar, doesn't mean I don't like fish!" Jonathan remarked.

I laughed. "I can be pretty fishy!" I said. "Maybe I'm more of a shrimp than a fish." The two men smiled.

"I have to get back to work," Jonathan said, "We may meet at the funeral." We shook hands and then Jonathan left.

"Jonathan is very orderly, almost prissy," Tom said. "Father John told me you were a bit crude, but friendly."

"I guess I could be described that way," I said. I looked at Tom who looked confused. He was a little bit afraid too. Tom's hand was shaking some.

"The idea of crude sex turns you on, doesn't it?" I asked. Tom nodded.

"I'm not rough," I said. "I just look it."

"Father John said you were really big?"

"That part of me is rough," I said. "I take my time, but it's filling, if that's what you mean. No training wheels for my cock."

"You've seen John's cock? It's the biggest I've taken," Tom said. "I loved it."

"Well, I'm a little longer and a lot thicker," I said. "To tell you the truth, I watched him fuck Rollie and I'm rough compared to that."

Tom leaned close to me. "Have you ever fucked a guy to an orgasm?" he whispered. "That's never happened to me."

"I'm not sure I've ever fucked a guy who didn't shoot off," I answered. "I like to fuck a guy until I see the cream."

"Jonathan doesn't like a mess," Tom whispered. "I've never shot off with him. I love getting fucked by Father John, but it's never been intense enough to get me off. I have the feeling sex can be more exciting. John was surprised Rollie could take yours."

"Do you think you could take mine?"

"Father John said your penis was so big it was almost gross," Tom said. "I live next door."

"Would you like to look at it before you try it on for size?"

Tom nodded. "Would you do that? You must think I'm . . ." I interrupted him.

"Curiosity doesn't bother me at all, as long as you're up front about it," I said. Tom looked relieved. We left the church and went to the Rectory next door. It was a big house. Tom explained Father John lived in an old farm three miles out of town. The church owned the Rectory, so he lived there for free. We went up to his bedroom. Tom pulled the shades. I started to undress. Tom just stood there. I stopped and began to undress him; he was shaking.

"Relax," I told him. "Calm down and let nature take its course." I hugged him and he stopped shaking.

"You must think I'm a fool," Tom said. "I'm a grown man. I shouldn't get this excited." He was too nervous to do anything, so I stripped him. I was getting hard, and when Tom saw my cock for the first time, all was well. Lust triumphed over fear. He saw, he sucked and then he tried to swallow it.

Tom was such an enthusiastic sucker, I wondered if he had lost interest in getting fucked. This wasn't a problem. I licked his cock head and tasted pre cum. We were the same height, so when we 69ed it was a perfect fit. As he sucked my cock, I pulled up his legs so I could inspect his ass. He was clean, but I could smell lubricant. I ran my tongue around his anus. It was pink and puffy. I forced my tongue into the middle of the pucker. It tasted of lube and pre cum.

Using my detective's skills, I guessed Father John had been in his ass earlier. Father John had cocked the pistol, but hadn't pulled the trigger. No wonder Tom was so desperate. I worked my tongue into his hole again. This time Tom tried to open up. He wanted it bad. I licked my finger and pushed it in deep enough to press his prostate. Tom moaned.

He was excited. "How do you want to fuck me?" Tom asked.

"What do you want?" I replied. He whispered to me, "Can you fuck me like a dog?" I smiled. That position gave me most control. I realized he wanted me to run things.

"You think you can take my cock?" I asked in a whisper.

He looked at my cock. "It's huge. I want it,"

"Wanting it and taking it isn't the same thing," I reminded him. "Once I'm in half way, it's really hard for me to stop. You may get it all whether you want it all or not."

Tom said. "Fuck me until I shoot. Fuck the cum from me!" He was true to his word. It wasn't easy for him. Tom tended to whimper and cry, but when I tried to pull out or even slowed up, he would beg me to keep on pushing.

Somewhere between seven inches and total penetration, Tom had a religious experience. Tom found god. Which god, I don't exactly know, but he found someone. He had his hands free orgasm and much more. Tom turned into a fuck-toy bottom pig, a quivering mass of sexually charged flesh.

I'm good about staying hard, but Tom's excitement was contagious. Over the next hour and a half, I must have penetrated him ten to fifteen times. I think I shot off five times, but it was hard to count. I fucked him every way possible, and then invented some new ways. His ass bonded to my cock.

After an hour of fucking, Tom and I relaxed. The drive to have an orgasm disappeared and it turned into pure pleasure. He was limp as a dishrag. He could still quiver and moan, but otherwise he had become a part of my sexual apparatus. The sensation turned from being a raging storm to a flowing brook of pleasure.

We calmed down and I almost fell asleep. Once and a while Tom would shiver. I pulled out.

"Did I tell you I wanted to get fucked?" Tom asked. I laughed.

"I think you mentioned it," I said. "You forgot to tell me when you had enough. I'm afraid you might get a callus on your sphincter." I went to the bathroom and got a wet towel. I squirted some lube on my finger and massaged his bloated anus. It was a puffy and abused. My sperm was drooling from his hole, so I wiped it up as I gently massaged the opening.

"I feel so empty," Tom whispered. My cock wasn't soft yet, so I nuzzled my cock head in the opening and played with it. I didn't fuck. I just played. He was so open now my cock head popped the sphincter a few times. We broke apart, showered and I went back to town.

I went to Aunt Edith's house to see what was up.

Part 6

Things were winding down at Edith's house. The State Police crew was finished and the Volunteer Firemen were cleaning the place up. Scooter wanted the place cleaned up before my Aunts saw it. Donnan saw me and waved me over to the RV.

"We got the official autopsy report. She was killed with a massive blow to the head from behind. It's a classic blunt instrument crime. She died instantly and literally didn't know what hit her," he said. "The Medical Examiner thinks she had been dead an hour or two before they cut her up. The fire followed that."

"It seems mighty odd," I said. "You would think that sort of thing would be done in the heat of rage or passion. Rage would seem to be the most probable cause, given Aunt Edith's personality."

"The Police chief came by here earlier," Donnan said. "He thinks the mutilation is a red herring. He knew some locals who like to cut up people, but it's before death."

"What was the blunt instrument?" I asked.

"We don't know, but we know it wasn't left in the house." Donnan said. "That is a problem. If it were a spontaneous act, it would have been left. Have you been looking into your Aunt's business affairs?"

"I have some info. She owned lots of property all over the place. I think most of it is considered worthless, but you can't be sure," I said. My cell phone rang. It was Mom. I was needed. Some relatives were coming and I had to be dressed. I went back to Scooter's farm, showered, dressed, and then went to the main house.

There were several cars in the yard with window stickers from my hometown. Inside were several of my mother's lady friends and one older man, Graham. Graham was about seventy and distinguished looking. My gaydar was totally silent. He was concerned about my Mother and Aunts. After ten minutes, I realized Graham and my Mother were more than friends.

I was shocked. I had been so use to thinking of my Mom as a widow. I hadn't considered she might have a boyfriend, not to mention a lover. Graham was about six feet tall and well spoken. He was the former superintendent of schools one of the neighboring counties of my hometown. I was surprised when another man entered the room. He was Graham's son, Carl, who had served as a chauffeur.

We all chatted politely. Graham didn't know what to think of me, but when conversation got to the murder and I gave them a clear update, Graham warmed up. Carl made a few comments and my gaydar went into overdrive. Carl looked like a pale copy of his father.

On the dining room table, Mom had a pile of deeds they had found in the bank box and in the house. I noticed they had put a drop cloth over the table since the documents were dirty. Mom was always neat. "There's so much," Mom said, "We're having a problem getting a grip on it." Carl started looking at the documents, then sat down and began to sort.

We discussed Edith's financial situation and I mentioned my meeting with the County Clerk, Jonathan. "Carl, why don't you go to the courthouse and look things up," Graham said.

"Just a minute," Carl said. "I've just about finished sorting them." I looked at the table. The documents were in neat piles. "Do you have a pad?" he asked. Fifteen minutes later, he rose from the table. The pad was covered in his notes.

"This pile is deeds for mines. Next to it are the purchases of mineral rights," he said as he pointed out the stacks of documents. "The third pile is for large farms or other big acreage parcels. The fourth pile is for properties in town. Let's go to the courthouse."

I volunteered to drive him. Carl was an accountant who worked with estates. It was clear he knew his stuff. When he met Jonathan, I realized the two men were soul mates. It was love at first sight. Deed books flew out of the safe and the computer churned out printed copies. Jonathan got his assistant, a pale, blond, young man name Elroy to get the assessed value of the properties.

I had to get back to my Mom. Jonathan said he'd be glad to drop Carl off at the funeral home later, if Carl wanted to get all the information. I knew I was the third wheel, so I returned home. There, we had a quick dinner of sandwiches and salads and went to the funeral home.

Aunt Becky mused that maybe she should take a last look at the body. Billy put the kibosh to that. "I'm really sorry ma'am, but the coffin is sealed," he said. "It would take a lot of work to open it." I didn't think this was true, but Becky accepted it. Rev. Pettigrew came, as did Tom, the organist.

Tom said he wanted to check the music with my Aunts. After he spoke with them, he came over to me. "I enjoyed this morning," he whispered. I said that I had enjoyed it too. "I have a friend who'd love to meet you," Tom continued whispering. "He's young, but a good boy."

"Boy?"

Tom smiled, "He's 24 and just got out of the Army," he said. "Timmy will be here with his Mom tonight. He was a member of the Choir. He was a bass at 14!" Tom moved on.

As Billy the funeral director had said, there was a good crowd. A few pretended to like Edith, but all were polite and sympathetic to my Mom and Aunts. We had several delegations from churches. She had run through churches at a good pace. Most didn't meet her standards for very long. As she got older, Edith got purer than pure. I heard a, "She was a sad and complex woman," from one group, and an "I hope she's found peace," from another. One group actually asked if Edith had remembered them in her will.

After an hour, a diminutive woman and her huge son came up to us. "Hello, I'm Edna Baker and this is my son, Timothy," she said in introduction. "I use to teach Sunday school with Edith. She wanted to save the world, you know. I told her she should be happy if she could help just one person, but that wasn't enough for her." Needless to say, Edna and my Aunts got on like gangbusters. I think while Edna knew Edith's faults, she also had genuinely liked her.

Timmy was at least 6'-4" and massive. He had a curly, black beard and was already well on the way to being bald, but he was oddly baby faced. He had clear, intensely blue eyes and a pink complexion. We talked. He had left the army a year earlier and worked for a surveyor.

"Have you by any chance run into a group called Capitol Exploration?" I asked, taking a shot in the dark.

"As a matter of fact, I have," Timmy said. "I've been doing quite a bit of work. It's not the usual. Most of our work is boundary surveys and deed work. Capitol's stuff is different. We're locating old mines."

"What do you mean?"

"Most of the mines closed 50 or 60 years ago," Timmy explained. "You can still find some of the bigger ones, but the smaller ones are lost. Monty is looking for them."

"Monty is Capitol's man?"

"Yep, he a nice guy too," Timmy said. "I've spent a lot of time tramping around the mountains for him. My boss says he pays top dollar." Timmy was young and wearing boxers. I could tell he had a nice package. He glanced at my crotch. Obviously, Tom had told him about my cock. Tim was getting excited.

"Any chance I could talk to you about this later?" I asked under my voice.

He smiled. "I live at home. Maybe we could meet at the diner later. It closes at 11:00 on Friday nights," he said. Then under his breath, he said, "Mr. Robinson said you were a good guy."

"Tonight's a possibility?" I asked, "Around ten after I take the ladies home?" Timmy nodded.

I was there at ten on the dot. Timmy was waiting at counter. The diner was otherwise empty. Andy was talking with Tim. Festus was washing dishes. Tim told me about his work with Capitol. I remembered some of the names he talked about were names of properties Edith owned.

Festus peaked out of the kitchen, saw Tim and smiled. Tim blushed. Wythetown was a small place, and the gay community was even smaller. Festus and Tim knew each other, but I didn't sense Andy knew we were all brothers.

Festus was finished with the dishes and Andy said he'd close up. We left with Festus. Tim treated Festus like a favorite younger brother. They were pals. "I'll drive Festus home," Tim said.

"Come home with me and we can have some desert." Festus said, "Ice cream! I made it myself."

"Festus is an ice cream fanatic," Tim explained. Festus lived in an apartment above the pharmacy. We went up a long, narrow stair. The stair was dingy, but the apartment was nice. It was a loft type open space with a bath and kitchen separating the sleeping area from the living. It was hot and Festus stripped off his shirt and turned on several ceiling fans. He went off to the bath to shower.

Festus joined us three or four minutes later. He was nude and drying off. "No air conditioning," he said. "I like being bare. You can't see in the windows. We're too high above the street." Tim stripped too and I joined them.

When I was naked, Fetus came over to me and fondled my cock. "Tim, Clydesdale has Godzilla's cock!" he said in explanation.

"Tom told me about it," Tim said. "It may sound odd, but I wanted to see it." He paused, "You must think I'm a jerk."

I smiled. "You aren't the first," I said. "There's nothing wrong with a little curiosity."

"It's not little," Festus remarked. We all laughed. By then, Tim was hard and I went down on him. I didn't know if Tim was a looker or a player, but I figured you can't go wrong sucking a cock.

It turned out Tim wasn't sure what he wanted. His sexual experiences were limited to Tom and Festus. He liked what he had done, but was uneasy about going further. Tim wasn't a size queen. He thought my cock was interesting and was more than willing to suck it, but didn't feel an urge to feel it in his ass.

Festus was another matter. He had seen me in action at Rollie's birthday party and wanted to get to know my cock more intimately. "Will you fuck me?" he asked me. "I like getting fucked."

"He's awfully big," Tim remarked. "It might not fit."

"You fuck me first, then Clydesdale." Festus said. He had a plan. Tim was covered in a pelt of curly black hair. At first, his cock was all but concealed in his bush. When he got hard, it was a massive member. Tim was hung thick, rather than long. He had a small cock head, and a bulbous shaft. The shaft tapered as it vanished in Tim's pubic bush, butt plug style.

Tim looked uncertain. He was shy.

"Hey, we're all boys here," I said, "I've seen it all before."

"I shoot easily," Tim said. "It's kind of messy."

"Tim shoots hard," Festus added, "It tickles my ass when he shoots." Tim may have wanted to hold back but he was a horny young man. He coated his cock with lubricant and Festus got on his hands and knees. Tim positioned his cock at Festus' hole and pushed.

Tim was gentle. It was clear he didn't want to hurt Festus. Tim's thick cock was no easy piece of meat, and he was trying to cushion the impact by going slow.

"I hope you don't mind some advice from an old fucker, but he'll enjoy it more if you shove it in fast," I said. "Don't be shy; just pop it through the hole." Tim looked uncertain, but he was the kind of kid who did what he was told. He thrust hard, and his cock vanished in Festus' love tunnel. Festus moaned in pleasure.

"Now, just stay still for a while and let him get used to it," I said.

"How long?" Tim asked.

"He'll let you know," I explained. "You're fully loaded, aren't you?"

"I'm afraid I am," he said sheepishly. "I'm sorry."

"There's nothing to be sorry about," I said. "We're here to drain our balls. The only question is, how much fun we can have working up to the climax." Festus had begun rotating his ass. Tim began to thrust in response to the movement. Tim was a pile driver and I got him to slow down a little.

It didn't take long for Tim to realize the advantages of the slow and easy approach to anal sex. Festus was an aggressive and generous bottom. He obviously loved it and wanted Tim to like as much as he did. When Tim slowed down, Festus began to rotate his ass and I could see him tensing his butt. He was trying to milk Tim's cock.

Tim had a hair trigger, but I got Festus to slow down when I sensed Tim was ready to pop. Festus was a quick learner, and soon they had it down to a science. Tim would work up to an orgasm, and Festus would slow him down. They went on for fifteen or so minutes before Tim finally blew. Tim had a full body orgasm. He shook, he shivered, and he twitched and moaned until his balls were drained. When he pulled out, I nosed my meat into Festus's cum filled chute.

I had watched the Police Chief fuck him at the party, so I knew Festus didn't mind the "slam, bang, thank you ma'am" school of fucking. Thompson was meaty, but not as a big as me. I figured Festus could take it if I took my time.

Festus was still on his hands and knees. I got four or five inches in and rested. He needed a breather. I leaned over him and got one hand on his cock and the other around his chest. He had a slightly furry chest and his cock was still hard. I lifted him up, so he was essentially sitting back on my cock. From this position, I figured his own weight would force my cock further up his ass.

Usually I need to add lube several times to get my cock in an ass, but Tim had filled Festus with his jiz and it was downright juicy. I like the cool feeling of lube, but Tim's man seed was hot and slippery. My legs were between Festus's, and I widened my stance, forcing his legs wider and opening his ass even more. Festus whimpered a little, but eventually he was fully impaled.

"You're in," I said.

"It's all in?" Festus whispered.

"Every inch."

"Damn!" he replied. "I can't believe I ate the whole thing!"

"You need to rest?"

"Just a little," he said. "I just need to catch my breath." When Festus said a little, he meant it. In less than a minute, he was squirming to get my cock into a better position. Tim was on the floor recovering from his orgasm. He rolled over and licked Festus's cock.

After a few minutes of this, I got on my back and Festus straddled me, then he sat on it. This turned out to be the perfect position for him. He had complete control in this position. Festus did what could only be described as a hula dance on my cock. I wasn't fucking him. His hole was massaging my cock.

Festus leaned over a few times to kiss me. Tim was watching and he took the opportunity to lick my balls. Half of my cock was in Festus's ass and the second time this happened, Tim's tongue licked my shaft and it felt as if he was trying to get it into the ass with my cock. This made Festus shoot off.

I knew Tim wanted to try my cock, but I somehow felt he wasn't ready. Tim was hard again, so I coated his cock with lube and sat on it, doing my imitation of Festus's fancy dance. As I had guessed, Tim's cock was a living butt plug and I had a good time. This time he popped quickly. Festus had said you could feel cum squirting from Tim's cock. I had thought this was an exaggeration, but it was true. I felt long squirts and an almost tickling sensation in my ass. I had a pretty spectacular hands-free orgasm because of this. A good time was had by all. I had to get back to the farm so we broke up. The next day was the funeral.

Part 7

The next day began when Daryl, Aunt Becky's son, and Liz, Ellen's daughter, arrived. I had been afraid Edith's nasty disposition had driven the close relatives away. Liz was with her son, Herb. Cousin Buddy also came with his kids, John and Cecilia, who were teenagers now. My Mom had been helping them since their Mom was murdered. There was bad blood between Daryl, Liz and Aunt Edith, so it was good they came to give their mothers some support.

The funeral was as good as it could have been. Rev Pettigrew put a lot of emphasis on the "all knowing, all understanding and all forgiving God." Mom and my Aunts liked that. The music was good. Tom was a spectacular organist and the old, war-horse type hymns sounded new again. There was a good crowd, mostly of older people. The Police Chief was there in uniform. The state troopers were in plain clothes. Some murderers like to go to the funeral of their victims. The Troopers were on watch.

Rollie had lined up some younger men to be the pallbearers. I sat with my Aunts since Graham had my mother under his wing. Jonathan assisted in the service. I saw Carl looking at him and recognized something much closer to love than I would have guessed.

The cemetery was two miles away. It was old and pretty. Edith had erected a tall obelisk by Uncle Edgar's grave. Everything was quiet, peaceful and dignified. It was a cool and pleasant day. We went to a local restaurant for lunch with Edith's friends and our relatives. Most of them were getting well up in years, only a few of my generation were there. In the afternoon, we talked. My Aunts were overwhelmed by the amount of work that needed to be done to settle the estate and to go though the house. They were tired and emotionally drained.

Daryl, Liz and Buddy had planned to go home after the funeral, but that was before Cecilia began to plan. "Since we're here, we might as well get as much done as we can and get it out of the way. We're free for the next couple of days. Why don't we see what we can do?"

"Everyone's tired," I said.

"It's just going to be hanging over everyone's head," Becky said. "It might be better to get it out of the way." Cecilia seemed to be a born leader of men and women. Soon everyone fell into line. That included Graham and Carl. Carl did estate work and he had no desire to go home as long as he had a chance to spend time with Jonathan. Graham said he'd do the legal work with the probate Judge while Carl went after the financial and real estate assets. Mom stayed close to Graham.

Daryl was a stockbroker in DC and joined Graham in dealing with the financial aspects of Edith's estate. I asked him if he knew anything about Capitol Exploration. He said no, but if there were a computer available, he would find out. I asked him to do that. Scooter had a computer in the doublewide. Liz and Herb joined the cleanup crew, with some bad grace. Liz hated Edith.

While Cousin Buddy was a deliberate and slow-moving farmer, his children were fireballs. After dinner, Cecilia drove me and her brother to the store to get cleaning and packing stuff. She had just got her license and wanted to show her newfound skills.

All the men stayed in Scooter's place and the women stayed with Elizabeth. It was crowded, but okay. I shared a bed with John and I would have to give the boy the first prize in a snoring contest. I don't know how the roof stayed on the double wide, given the snoring. Fortunately, I was so tired, it didn't make any difference.

We were up at the crack of dawn the next day and went off to the house with my Aunts before breakfast. Cecilia pulled some tubs onto the lawn and we started washing. She cleaned the china and small stuff. John went for the furniture.

John was built like his father and was strong as an ox. He was into bodybuilding, and nothing was too heavy for him to move. At 17 he was about as masculine as a kid his age could be. He also was a flaming heterosexual. I soon found out girls loved him and he loved them. John wasn't conventionally good looking, but he had an air.

I was going to get some breakfast from the diner, but that wasn't necessary. Bob and Sally Smith appeared and came over to see what was going on. When Sally found out we hadn't had breakfast, she went off to solve the problem. She was a good cook. Bob joined us cleaning. He also put up a small tent, so there would be shade. Eventually several neighbors joined us as did their teen-age children. Scooter and two other volunteer firemen joined us later. They knew a lot about smoke and water damage.

Cecilia was petite and pretty, energetic and outgoing. She was so energetic I was afraid she might have a problem. Her mother had spectacular mood swings. I talked to Buddy about it and he said he had taken her to a doctor. The doctor said he was just energetic, not manic-depressive.

Once we started working, Liz got in better humor. She had married a Catholic and that was the sin of sins to Edith. Herb was 23 or 24 and shy, but a hard worker. I was amazed at how much we got done.

One of the neighbors had a truck and he took several loads to the dump. There was no way to save most of the upholstered furniture. The acrid smell of the fire was over powering. There were several old pieces that could be stripped bare and redo. The rest was junk. Herb and I were tossing an armchair onto the truck when a letter fell out. It had been stuck in the pillows. The envelope said it was from Resource Management Inc. The letter was still inside.

The letter said Resource Management would investigate the potential of mineral and oil rights for a modest fee. The fee was $10,000.00. I knew Aunt Edith well enough to know that wasn't modest in her opinion. There was no chance in hell she would jump at that. Edith had written a note on the back. "Lou will do it for $3,000 if I pay him in cash."

I know a clue when I find it, I called Donnan and told him about it, and then I called Daryl. I asked him to look up Resource Management while he was investigating Capitol Exploration. They day turned out to be a good one. Mom and my Aunts found many heirlooms they thought had been lost. It was like a family reunion in many respects, and I also got to meet some of the neighbors.

By late afternoon we were bushed, but had done a lot. One of the neighbors was having a cook out for local teenagers at a nearby lake. Cecilia and John were invited. They were fast workers and had made friends with several locals. They would spend the night at a cabin there. This would reduce the overcrowding at Elizabeth's and simplify the sleeping arrangements at the doublewide.

We were all a bit ragged looking, so I took everyone to the diner for dinner. The dress code there was informal. It was a hit. Andy was a good cook. His special for the day was souvlaki, and my Aunts loved that. It had been a slow day at the diner and we made his day.

My Mom and Aunts went back to Elizabeth's house. The guys went to Scooter's doublewide. It was hot inside. "Why don't we go to the swimming hole and cool off while this place cools?" Scooter suggested.

"No trunks," Daryl complained.

"Shit, boy! You're in the country here!" Scooter exclaimed, "We're all born with our trunks. Haven't you skinny dipped before?"

"Not since I was a kid," Daryl said. "I spent a summer with Uncle Jake and I don't think he owned swimming trunks."

"As I recall, when he was at home, zipping your zipper was considered formal wear!" I said.

"He tended to wear his pants an inch or two below his pubic hair, as I recall," Buddy said.

"Mom said he was a character," Herb added. "I only met him once. She seemed to think he was a bad influence."

"He was a good guy," I said, "When my Dad died he was really helpful. He was a lot of fun too."

Daryl laughed. He glanced at me and I realized he had the same experience with Jake as I did. Jake had been my guide in the ways of man sex. "I wouldn't describe it as good clean fun, but it sure was fun," Daryl added, "It was one hell of a summer vacation." We trooped off to the swimming hole, stripped and jumped in. It was a spring fed pond and the water was cool and refreshing.

I was doing the dog paddle across the pond when Herb swam up to me. "I kind of thought from the way Mom talked, Uncle Jake was a dirty old man," Herb said.

I treaded water. "If she thinks that about Uncle Jake, what in hell does she think about me?" I asked.

Poor Herb blushed. "When she married Dad, she got big into religion. In some ways I think it was to get back at Aunt Edith and prove she could be a good Christian as a Catholic," Herb said. "Even Dad thought she took it too far."

"They're divorced now," I said. "That must have set her back."

"He's a nice guy. Dad told me Mom gave up on sex," Herb explained. "He wasn't going to become a monk at age 40. Mom's still afraid I might have sex for non procreative purposes."

"Shit, that's the only kind of sex I have," I said.

"Mom guessed that," Herb said. He paused. "It's the only kind of sex I have too," he whispered. "You like guys?" he asked.

"That's my poison."

"I've been having some non procreative sex too," Herb admitted. "With guys."

"You liked it?"

"I guess I did," Herb replied.

"I you just guessed you did, you're doing it wrong," I said. "Maybe you need lessons?" Glancing over to the other side of the pond, I saw Daryl, Buddy and Scooter in a close huddle. I knew there was action under the placid surface of the pond. I looked down into the clear water. Herb was hard. That seemed a good sign.

"It's time for beer!" Scooter yelled. We got out of the water. Looking around I could see no one was exactly soft. Buddy and Herb were fully erect. Herb looked relieved when he saw Buddy's erection. We grabbed our clothes and went back to the double wide, still naked.

Buddy was a middle-aged, hairy, ginger bear with an uncut, beer can style cock. Daryl was tall and thin, with a long, thin cock. It was sticking out at 45 degrees to his body. Herb was going to be hairy, like me when he got older. He had a runner's body and was toned rather than muscular. He had a tree trunk type cock, with a small head and shaft that grew thicker as I got nearer his body. Herb had to have the hairiest crotch I had ever seen. He was uncut and much of his skin was covered in hair. He must have had some balls somewhere in the thicket.

"I'm tired as hell," Scooter said, "but I wouldn't mind a little fun before I get to bed. Anyone who feels like playing can join me in my bedroom."

Buddy jumped up. "I'm game," he said. "Damn, I'm horny as hell."

"Is there anyone here who liked to get fucked?" Daryl asked. "The last time I did it was with Uncle Jake when I was 18. He told me I was good at it."

"I like it all. I'm a great top, if you like them big, but I'll bottom for a cousin." I said.

"Would you do it for me?" Herb asked. "I've never done it."

"Top or bottom?" Daryl asked.

"As a matter of fact, neither," Herb replied. "I'd like to try it. Clydesdale can guys really take your cock?"

"Some can," I said. "Scooter likes it. Buddy will take it if he's horny enough. We need to stop talking and get down to business." We all went to Scooter's bedroom. It turned out Scooter had his eye on Daryl and the two were 69ing as soon as the found the bed. Buddy was interested in Herb, so they went at it.

I was unoccupied, so I decided to play utility. I got out a tube of lubricant. I did Scooter's ass first. I knew he liked to bottom and I had some experience with his ass before. I squirted some on my finger then worked it into his hole. From the 69 position, Daryl watched my finger massage Scooter's hole, and then goes in. I got two fingers on the dark side and then found his prostate. Scooter loved it, but Daryl was turned on. I could tell he was excited. When I massaged Scooter's prostate, Daryl could taste the cock react.

I moved on to Daryl. He said he wanted to top, but I recalled Jake always wanted you to be able to reciprocate. Daryl jumped a little when I touched his buns for the first time. Then he moved his leg so I could get to his ass. He was really tight, but I took my time. It took maybe five minutes to get a finger in deep enough to press his magic nut.

Once I did that, Daryl sighed and opened wide. I could have gotten my entire hand in his ass if I was into that. I figured Uncle Jake had blazed the trail and Daryl was filled with fond memories. Buddy was next.

Buddy liked to bottom, but he was hard to open up. His ass was tight and it resisted penetration. Once you were in it was a great experience for the top. His ass was vice-like tight. It grabbed your cock and held it until you came. For a long time I was worried he didn't enjoy it as much as his tops did. I thought he didn't have a climax. It turned out Buddy usually had a hands free event early in a fuck session, but he didn't lose his erection until you pulled out. Buddy loved it. I took a while, but I got him lubed up.

Herb was an unknown quantity. He had watched me lubricate the other man and he knew what was coming. He was kissing Buddy and when it was his turn, he pulled up his legs and spread the wide so his hole was open. He was more than receptive. I swirled the lube around his hole and slipped a finger into his ass without much resistance. Herb's prostate was deep, but in full operating order. I was playing with it as I sucked Herb's cock when Daryl made a sneak attack from the rear on me.

Being a bottom isn't my best suit, but I try to be accommodating. A friend told me he thought of me as a social bottom, willing to take a cock at a party just to be part of the action. I wasn't lubricated, but Daryl was. He had seven inches, but his knob was the only part of his cock with any heft.

Daryl's head popped in effortlessly. The shaft slid deep into my ass. I felt an incredible rush of sensation. The cock must have hit every hot spot in my ass. Herb's ass was on the edge of the bed, with his legs drawn up and spread. I had two fingers in his ass, one on each side of his prostate. Bent over, I was sucking Herb's cock as I squeezed his prostate. Each time I squeezed, Herb would ooze some precum.

It must have been coincidence, but every time Herb oozed, Daryl thrust deep. It was a perfect coordination of oral and anal sensations. I was in heaven.

"Damn, I'd forgotten how good this is!" Daryl moaned. "Shit, I need to pull out, or I'll shoot." He pulled out.

"Too close?" Scooter asked.

"I'm out of practice," Daryl said. "Would you believe the last ass I was in was Jake's? That was 30 years ago."

"It's a bit like riding a bike, ain't it?" Buddy remarked. Buddy slipped his cock into my hole. Buddy usually bottomed, so I guessed he was inspired by the moment.

At 9:00 that night, I got a call from my office. All hell had broken loose. Roosevelt, my right hand man had been shot. He had interrupted a robbery attempt at a convenience store. He had saved the clerk, but took three bullets in the chest. One was near his heart. I had a few beers, so I went to bed. I woke at 5:00 and drove to Richmond. Buddy would take my Aunts home; Graham took my mother back.

Part 8

The next three weeks were busy and I couldn't think of my Aunt's murder. I had to fill in for Roosevelt. Roosevelt turned the corner a day after I got back, but it was going to be a while before he got up to full speed. He wanted to come back in a week, but I knew that was stupid. Our work was dangerous and when someone was hurt, we took care of them.

Adding to the confusion one of our night watchmen, Old Barney was killed. Barney was a nice old man who looked sweet, but was hard as nails. He went to places that had problems. He looked like an easy mark, but had a direct connection to our office. He was at a gated condo project that was having a problem with burglars.

He saw them getting away and they shot him. Barney got the license number down before he died. He was professional to the end. We paid for the funeral; his family was on the west coast. Some cousins came. I was getting to be good about funerals.

The City police treated the funeral as if Barney was one of their men. We had an honor guard and policemen from all over the state. That was important for our men. They didn't get much respect, and they appreciated it. Barney was also listed as the arresting officer. It was a good collar. The buglers at the condo were just the tip of an iceberg. The entire gang was rolled up and burglaries dropped by 20% in one day. Barney's murder upped the profile of the burglars, so the Judges showed no leniency to the gang members.

I got a call a few days after the funeral from my cousin, Daryl. He had been doing research on Capitol Exploration and Resource Management. Capitol was a real company, but low profile. They were the advanced guard of oil and gas exploration. They did the nosing around in advance of the big boys.

"If it looks like a good prospect, they may take options on good properties before the word gets out," he explained.

"You think they were looking at Aunt Edith's property?"

"I talked with one of my friends who is an energy analyst," Daryl said. "There is interest in old mining properties, especially if they have been abandoned for a long while. They figure the properties haven't been explored by any modern investigating methods. That would seem to fit Edith's properties perfectly."

"What about the other operation, Resource Management?"

"A different kettle of fish all together," my cousin said. "They are bottom feeders. Essentially, they spy on Capitol and try to sneak their way in. They are associated with a bunch of wildcatters in Texas. Resource doesn't do any exploratory work on its own. They steal other companies work."

"Nice work if you can get it," I said.

"Some of Capitol's men have been assaulted and one or two shot at," Daryl said. "Given the state of the energy markets now, there's a lot of money involved if you get the right properties."

"Edith owned most of the mining properties in the area, didn't she?"

"It sure looks that way to me."

I took this information and went to my geek squad. They had been involved in Roosevelt's shooting and in Barney's death, but they were eager to show their computer search skills. With my cousin's information, they searched out employees and the executive staff of the two companies.

Jonathan Snelling, the chief geek came back to me two days later. Capitol's board was made up of lesser functionaries of big oil and gas companies. "As far as I can tell, these are men and women who have been marked as on the way up, but are still little known," he said. "The other one is made up of front men only. The Chairman is Rosa Martin. She's legal secretary for a law firm in Dallas. The treasurer is a new employee of a law firm in Fort Worth."

"Protected by rules of legal confidentiality?" I asked.

"That's the hope," Jonathan said, "I'm not sure it would hold up in court, but it might be enough to hold things up for a year or two in a trial situation. The real executives will be in Brazil or some island in the Caribbean by then."

"Can you find out more?"

"I rather think we can," Jonathan. "It may take some time, but eventually the cash needs to be in the hands of the real owners of the company. By the way, Charley found an ad for the company on a soldier of fortune web site. Wanted real men for work in Southwest Virginia. The listed contact was Resource Management. There was a phone number."

"Can I see that?"

Jonathan printed it out. Sometimes you're good, and sometimes you're just lucky. This was my day to be lucky. Reading between the lines, you could tell they were after none too bright rednecks. Playing that role was my strong suit.

I called the number listed in the advertisement. I did it from a phone in the lobby a flophouse. I have quite an accent, so they thought I was the genuine article. I was a bit cagy about having a Social Security number and they seemed to like that.

They told me to be at a motel in Roanoke in a week. I said that was fine with me. I went to my barber and told them to give me the red neck special. I had a beard that made me look like the Czar. Twenty minutes later, I had a Fu Manchu and a ponytail. When I left the barber, a young couple crossed to the other side of the street to avoid me. I couldn't ask for better.

I had a set of poorly forged documents that made me Willard Dolan. It was close enough to my real name that I could respond to it automatically. I sent off to Roanoke in a 23-year-old rust encrusted Mustang.

I got to the motel room and knocked. There were two guys inside. One was a businessman named Mark Jones, the other was a "Field Representative" named Sid. Mark was slimy; Sid looked deranged. The room smelled of air freshener. It tried to cover the smell of piss. The Motel was rock bottom. There was also an under smell of weed.

Mark interviewed me. I think Sid had smoked a few too many and he seemed to be daydreaming. Mark said they were an energy research firm looking for men who wanted to be in on the ground floor of new discoveries in oil and gas.

I volunteered I had heard there was money in oil. That established I didn't spend much time reading the Wall Street Journal. I thought I might have a hard time convincing them I was a real red neck. They had no question about that. My job would be to watch and see what their competitor was doing. "That's all?" I said.

"That's it. The salary is modest, but if you get some good info, we have a profit sharing program," Mark said. I figured the modest salary explained the $35.00 a night bedroom. They discussed benefits.

I looked uneasy. "Too tell you the truth, I'm not too interested in benefits," I said. "My ex has a court order for back child support payments. Cash and no questions asked is what I like."

"How much are you in the hole for?" Mark asked.

"The last time she caught me it was $150,000.00. Every time I fucked the bitch, she dropped another one. I skedaddled," I explained.

"Damn, I'm only behind $50,000.00," Mark said. "How'd you do that?"

"I vamoosed when she was in the hospital with my fifth," I said, chuckling. "I've never paid one yet."

"Well, I can understand your situation," Mark said. "When can you get working?"

"Is tomorrow too soon?"

"That's the attitude I like," Mark said. He took out his wallet and gave me a $100.00 bill. "Think of this as a retainer." I took it and thanked him. I left.

The $100.00 surprised me. I wondered how many men took the cash and left, or came in the next day so wasted, they couldn't function. When you were recruiting scum, it might be a good way to get rid of the worst of them.

I showed up the next morning. Sid was there with three other men. We would be the team, Sid said. There was a kid named Sean, a Mexican named Juan, and the head of our team was a guy named Halsey. Halsey was tall and might have been good looking if he didn't drink so much. Sean looked stupid, and Juan was just out of it. I don't think he could speak English well.

Someone knocked at the door. Sid opened it and another man entered. "Men, this is Reggie," Sid said. "He's another member of your group." Reggie looked a little like Gabby Hayes. His eyes were bloodshot and I guessed getting up that morning had been an iffy thing.

We were going to go to the Wythetown area, but would be camping. "We don't want anyone to know you are there," Sid explained. If we found something, we were to report it to him. I was the only one to have a car other than Halsey. I took Reggie, Sean, and Juan. Apparently, the executive staff didn't want to associate with the peasants.

We drove way into the forest. Reggie and Sean were talkative. "Damn, I came close to missing out on this," Reggie said. "I keep on thinking I've put demon rum behind me and then he makes a sneak attack!"

"The god damned cashier carded me," Sean complained.

"I don't have that problem," Reggie said. "I should be retired now, but I'm still living hand to mouth."

"Is that demon rum striking again?" I asked.

Reggie looked at me, annoyed. Then he smiled. "That's part of it, bad luck's another part, and being just plain stupid a few times explains the rest," he said. "What's your story?"

"50% bad luck, 50% stupid," I said.

Sean laughed. "100% stupid here," he said. "I wasn't much into book learning, and it caught up with me," he said. "I got fired from a fucking 7-11. Do you believe that, a 7-11?"

"Maybe our luck has changed," I said. "It's sure about time for me."

The campsite was deep in the woods. The site was selected more for its seclusion than for any other reason. There were two tents, one for Halsey and Sid when he visited. The other tent was for us. It was a nice tent, new and clean. It could be left mostly open to the air or sealed up in bad weather. There was a porto-potty type thing, but I thought the bushes were better.

I thought we were hired to follow Capitol Exploration men. I was wrong. We had property maps and we were to find property stakes. Where Capitol was interested in the land, they added their own marker. We were to find these and mark the maps and remove Capitol's marker. It was a classic land swindler's game.

We had sophisticated GPS equipment that made it easy to find the corner points. It would have been easy if there wasn't topography, a dense forest and if the property maps were correct. It was rough work.

I went off with Sean and Juan. Sid and Halsey took Reggie. Juan was from the jungles of southern Mexico and had no problem with underbrush. Sean thought he was at summer camp. It was a hot day. By noon Juan and Sean were shirtless, I was in a tee shirt. Sean was thin and well built. He had long straggly hair and a half hearted effort at a beard. He had a patch of hair in the middle of his chest and a treasure tail that disappeared into his jeans.

Juan was smooth and had straight, black hair and a bushy mustache. He was short and very muscular. His jeans were tight and he seemed to have a nice package. We found six property stakes, none of which had Capitol's markers next to them. I was disappointed, but when we got back to camp, we found out the other group had found nothing.

Sid went off to town. He was going to do more research and told us to try again. He would return in a day or two with more information. He left. We were hot and very dirty. There was a stream nearby as well as a small pond with a deep area behind a small waterfall. It was about three feet deep in middle. We stood looking at the water. No one wanted to make the first move.

I took off my tee shirt, dropped my pants, took off my boots and shoes and jumped in my birthday suit. Juan and Sean were right behind me. Halsey and Reggie joined us later. "I haven't been bare in a river in years," Reggie said. "I hope you don't mind seeing a fat old man's body."

"A body's a body," I said, "I hope you don't mind a hairy redneck."

"What in hell is hanging between your legs, Clydesdale?" Sean asked. "Is that fucker real?"

"It's a prize winner," Reggie said.

"We all get the cards we're dealt," I said. Juan just stared at my cock. Halsey looked at it whenever he thought I was looking the other way. Sean had a long, thin, uncut appendage. His balls hung very low. Juan had compact and possibly meaty equipment. He too was uncut.

Reggie has a big, well-filled ball sack, with his large mushroom sitting on it. There was no indication of a cock shaft at all. He was uncut, but the head was big enough to part the skin and I saw his slit. He was a bear like man and I expected that. Halsey was well endowed. I suspected he had a hard time getting it up. He wasn't in good shape, and he always smelled of booze. He must have had a bottle in his backpack.

All of the men seemed interested in my cock. That would certainly help the nights to go by quickly. Dinner was some sort of trail food. It was a hot night and we were wearing only shorts and bug spray. We went to our tent after eating. Halsey went off to his alone, I assume to drink.

I was horny so I dropped my shorts. "I hope you guys don't mind if I sleep naked?" I asked.

"Shit, if I was hung like you, I'd be naked all the time," Sean replied. Reggie was wearing boxers, but when he sat on his cot, he stripped them off. "Damn I'm stiff," he moaned. "I haven't had so much exercise in years."

"Lie down and I'll give you a massage," I said. Reggie was more than willing. My cock was at Reggie's eye level and he made no effort to turn away. As he looked at it, he licked his lips. So far, so good I thought. I began rubbing him down.

"It feels good," Reggie said. Then he whispered, "The view is nice too." Sean was giving Juan an English lesson. Juan was smart I think and he picked up things easily.

I leaned over Reggie and whispered. "It tastes better than it looks."

"I guessed that," he replied.

After a while, I decided to change my position. By now, the sun was down and it was dim in the tent. "I need to get my back into this," I said as I climbed onto his ass. The view wasn't as good for Reggie from this position, but it was better for my cock. As I massaged Reggie, my cock was rubbing on his ass. He seemed to like it.

I hoped to have a little cock action before the night was over. My bet was Reggie would slip out of bed when Sean and Juan were asleep and give me a blowjob. Meanwhile I was getting into the massage. I could feel Reggie relaxing as I worked on his muscles.

The English lesson continued, but Sean and Juan kept an eye on me and Reggie. They couldn't see much, but they were suspicious. Eventually they got up and came over to watch. By then I was hard.

"Are you enjoying yourself?" Sean asked.

"Moving in that direction," I said. "Are you interested?"

"I wouldn't mind watching." Sean said.

"This kind of fun ain't a spectator sport," I told him. "You can either join in, or go to bed."

"I don't know. . ."

"You may not know, but your cock sure does," I said. "You're sporting a nice one. So is Juan." Young guys are always ready. They can try to be cool, but cocks aren't into cool at all. Cocks are always in the get naked, get hard and get it on mode.

Sean looked down and his jockey's were tented. "Are you gay?" he asked.

"I sure as shit am, but I don't want to marry you, or Reggie for that matter," I said. "I just want to get my rocks off. Do you guys want to join us?"

Sean didn't answer. He just stripped of his jockeys and exposed his rock hard cock. He looked at me, but when he got closer, Reggie got his cock. Reggie had no problem sucking, and Sean liked to be sucked. All was well.

Juan just looked on and stroked his cock. He gave Sean a look. Sean backed away from Reggie. Juan came forward and Reggie sucked him. Everyone was with the program. Sean watched Reggie licking Juan's cock and then he bent over and licked my cock head.

"It's kind of sweet," he said.

"Precum," I said. "It's 100% redneck cock jelly." He went back to my cock and this time he took my entire cock head in his mouth. Sean had found something he liked. By the time the night was over, I realized there wasn't a whole lot Sean didn't like. He may not have been gay, but he sure liked sex with men. Juan liked it too, but he was more reserved.

Reggie liked it all. I think it had been a long time since Reggie had sucked on a young man's cock. He was in heaven. After sucking them and me, Reggie volunteered he wouldn't mind a cock in his ass. It only took a few seconds for Sean to get into Reggie's ass and a minute later, he had shot his load. I think his orgasm lasted longer than the fuck.

Juan stepped up to the plate. He wasn't as long as Sean's, but he was a lot thicker. Reggie moaned as Juan's meat stretched his ass. Once Juan was in Reggie's warm and tight chute, he lost his reserve. Fucking was Juan strong suit. He was good at it.

I thought Juan would shoot off as quickly as Sean, but he had stamina. He was a natural born fucker and he varied his pace. He would slow down when he was close to shooting, and when the urge passed he speeded up again. He fucked for a good half hour. Reggie loved it.

Finally, Juan shot off and pulled out.

"Are you done, or can you take another one?" I asked. Reggie nodded.

"Can you really take that horse cock?" Sean asked. "He'll split you in half."

"I'll take the chance," Reggie muttered.

I nosed my cock into his ass, and pushed slowly. I was surprised his ass was still tight. There was a pint or two of cum in Reggie's ass. Cum lubricated the chute, so it was both slippery and tight, no wonder Juan liked it so much. Reggie had no problem with my cock either.

I hadn't thought Reggie was exactly a virgin, but when he took my cock with such ease, I realized he was experienced. It's nice to be appreciated, and as Reggie got into it, I got into it. I fucked him pile driver style for a good fifteen minutes. I struck gold and we shot off together. Sean watched us go at it with a look of awe on his face.

The next day was a replay of the day before, except I was with Halsey. It was hotter and longer but we had slightly better luck and found four corner posts to a property. We got back to the camp and had another poor dinner. Sid had not reappeared and Halsey was getting really antsy. I knew the signs, the liquor cabinet was empty and Sid was to refill it.

I wanted to go swimming after dinner. Poor Halsey was in a state by then, but went with me. The other guys didn't want to be with Halsey and they stayed in the tent. The cool water calmed him down some. "Tense?" I asked.

"I need a drink," he said.

"I kind of guessed that," I said. "I recognized the signs."

"I was doing good until . . ." Halsey said.

"Until what?"

"Never mind, just don't cross Sid," Halsey said. "He's a bad man, a real bad man." Halsey was shivering. I don't know if it was withdrawal or Sid.

"Relax," I said.

"I can't relax," Halsey said.

"I bet I can get you relax," I said.

Part 9

Halsey was still up tight. I massaged his shoulders. He relaxed a little. It took a while but he finally calmed down. We chatted and he told me about his life. He had been a geologist with a family and a career. "I fucked up bad," he said. "I almost had it back together again when I got this shit ass job."

"The job sounds okay to me," I said.

"That's all it is," he said. "It sounds okay, but it's just table scraps. The hope is they can gum up the works for one of the real exploration companies and get a settlement in a law suit."

"No profit sharing?"

Halsey laughed. "No chance," he said. "It's just a line to feed a redneck."

"I like you too."

He looked up at me. "Sorry about that," he said. "I didn't mean it that way. I can be an asshole."

"Shit, everyone can be an asshole sometime," I said. I kept on massaging his shoulders and he continued to talk. "You were on the wagon for a while?"

"Five years," Halsey said.

"What knocked you off?"

"It was a month or so ago," he said. He was quiet. "I don't want to go there."

I didn't want to press it, so I continued rubbing his back. His cock was beginning to firm up. "Looking good," I said.

"Sorry about that," Halsey said.

"I've got no problem with hard cocks," I said.

"You've got a nice one," he said. "I have a problem getting up."

"Not tonight," I said. I reached over and stroked his cock. A bead of pre cum emerged. "Working up a head of steam?"

"I guess I am," he said.

"I can help out with it, if you want?" I asked. Halsey didn't say anything. I took that as a yes. I licked his cock head. He twitched and shot a single glob of cum into my mouth.

"You are ripe," I said.

"It's been a long while," Halsey said. "It felt good." Apparently, it was a single shot, so I went back to his cock. He just sat there without reacting. His cock was drooling pre cum non-stop, so I knew he enjoyed it.

Fifteen minutes later, he let loose. I have no idea when he had last shot off, but there must have had a month's supply of cum saved up. I sucked and swallowed, then did it again. His cum was creamy and thick. He stopped shooting, but I continued to suck and coaxed more seed from his balls. More came then the drooling stopped. Halsey's cock stayed hard, so I continued.

Five or ten minutes later, Halsey had a second major orgasm. It wasn't as big as the first, but it was still good.

"I don't believe I did that," Halsey moaned.

"Believe it," I said. "You got more cream stored up?" Halsey didn't answer, so I kept on sucking. A half hour later, he had a third orgasm.

"Do I need to suck you?" Halsey whispered.

"Do you like to suck cock?" I asked.

"Never done it," he said. "I owe you."

"You don't owe me anything," I said. "Some of the boys here like to suck. To tell you the truth, you're the first triple header I've ever had. I enjoyed it. Have you been sucked before?"

"Once when I was in college," he replied. "It was okay, but nothing like you. I'm not too experienced, but I would guess you're good at it?"

"You'd guess right."

Halsey went off to his tent. I returned to mine. Reggie was still awake and I slipped into his ass again. This time we didn't have an audience. It was just Reggie's ass and my cock. This time his ass opened and took it effortlessly. His ass quivered in excitement as I pushed in. I must have fucked him for a half hour or so and then I shot off and fell asleep.

The next day I went with Halsey again. It was more productive. When we got back to camp, we found a note from Sid. He wrote he was going to do some research in D.C. He would be back in several days.

He left some supplies, but no booze. Halsey was looking shocked. He was depending getting a new supply. I was feeling sorry for Halsey. I saw Reggie knew what Halsey was going through. I decided to make dinner. There wasn't much to work with, but I made a good meal. That was appreciated by all the guys. I'm not a good cook but I was a hell of a lot better than the other men.

Halsey was getting the shakes, but the food helped. It was a hot day so we went to the stream to cool off. Halsey joined us this time. The water was cool and pleasant. We had a good time. Halsey was a bit standoffish, but when he got out of the water, he was sporting a hard cock. That made a friend of Sean. Sean wasn't the shy type and soon he deep throated it. Halsey was well hung, but more long than thick. Sean had no problem with it.

I was with Juan and Reggie. Juan was sucking Reggie, so I decided to help myself to Juan's meat. His cock twitched when my lips touched it, but he didn't shoot. I knew he was cocked and ready to shoot, so I was careful. You didn't need to be too careful though. He had a recharge time of ten minutes. When I was his age, I could shoot off four or five times a day. I wondered if Juan had a limit. I was pretty sure Sean didn't have a limit. He was one horny cocksucker.

Everyone had a good time. After a few minutes, everyone was relaxed and playing. Halsey had been uneasy about sucking me, but he had no problem sucking Sean. When I say he had no problem sucking, I mean no problem.

Halsey was like a starving man who found himself at a banquet. Maybe he liked younger men, or perhaps a middle-aged fur ball wasn't his vision of the sexual partner of his dreams. He hit it off with Sean. Later he got it on with Juan too.

We sucked our way into the night. Eventually Halsey worked his way to me. He looked at me sheepishly. "This cock sucking can kind of grow on you," he said as he leaned over to suck me.

"I see you got the hang of it," I said. He had a little trouble taking my cock, but he was working at it. I appreciated the effort.

The next day Halsey was feeling better. I have always been of the opinion lots of sex can dent the edge of alcoholic withdrawal. Halsey was surprised that he was sporting first-rate woodie for the first time in years. All of his equipment was in working order, even if a bit rusty. Sean may have inspired a rebirth of sexual interest in him. I went with Reggie and Halsey took the two younger men.

Reggie and I had a long time to talk as we were in no rush to find more property lines. "Halsey had a good time last night." I said.

"He seemed to get into the swing, didn't he?" Reggie replied, "I feel sorry for him. I've been there. I know what he's going through."

"He told me he had been clean for a couple of years," I said. "What pushed him out of the wagon?"

"It was something bad." Reggie said. "I don't know exactly, but I think someone died. I think it involved a woman maybe. We tied one on one night and that's what I could make out."

"You weren't as drunk as he was?"

"Shit, no one could have been as drunk as he was," Reggie replied chuckling. "That boy was a hollow leg when it comes to rot-gut vodka. He's a nice guy I think. I really need the money. There's no way I'm qualified for the job. He knew that."

"Does Sid show up often? He's the boss."

"Sid's active some times, and sometimes he's really laid back," Reggie said. "When they interviewed me, I had to take a piss. There was a packet of white powder in a shaving kit in the bathroom. Halsey doesn't shave."

"That would explain mood swings," I said. "Was it coke, or heroin?"

"I'm not into that stuff myself. I favor the old vices, booze and fornication," Reggie said. "From the way Halsey talked it might have been higher powered. Crack maybe? Crystal Meth?"

"Damn, I hate new fangled drugs. I haven't even tried the old ones," I said. "It makes me feel old."

"If you're worried about looking old, don't look in the mirror," Reggie said. We laughed.

"Thank God you can still fuck like a rabbit when you're over the hill," I said. "I've got the cock of a fifteen-year-old."

"I've got the ass," Reggie said. "I don't want you to get a big head, but your cock sends me to the moon. I'd forgotten I could feel that much."

"I have a warm spot for size queens," I said.

"I hate to tell you, but I wasn't a size queen until I met you," Reggie said. "You converted me." He looked at me. "You aren't one of us, are you?"

"What do you mean?"

"You ain't a fuck up," Reggie said, "You're after something."

"Does that bother you?"

"I hope you're after Sid," Bernie said. "I'd hate for anything bad to happen to Halsey."

"I hope he's all right," I said. "I think he's a nice guy." Things were falling into place. Sid was a likely suspect and his drug problem might explain the brutality. Knowing and proving isn't the same thing. I might be able to get Halsey to turn Sid in, but I know a bad witness when I meet one. A good defense attorney could turn Halsey into Jell-O in ten minutes.

Sid returned that evening. He brought booze and Halsey couldn't resist. Sid and Halsey stayed to themselves. Sid gave us more detailed maps and we went over them and went to bed. Gunshots woke me an hour later. Sid was all hopped up and he was shooting into the air and screaming like a banshee. It took a few seconds for us to realize he was having hallucinations.

Armed men with delusions are bad. We were hiding in our tent. I could hear Sid screaming, but there was no sound from Halsey.

"You can't get away. I'll get you!" Sid screamed then he ran off into the woods. I got up and raced over to their tent. Halsey was under his cot not moving. I felt his pulse. He was alive. I grabbed him and dragged him to our tent.

"It's time to get out of Dodge," Sean said. My car was about a quarter of a mile away. It seemed Sid was off in the other direction. Halsey had a bump on his head, but it was clearly better to get away than to figure out exactly how badly he had been hurt.

Sean and Juan carried Halsey as we ran for the car. It was a dark night, but we made it. I was afraid Sid might have disabled the rust bomb, but it was fine. As I turned it on, we heard a gunshot, but it wasn't that close. We got away.

I didn't know exactly where we were, but we came to a major road in fifteen minutes. Five minutes later, we found a mileage sign. Wythetown was 22 miles away. Sean took the wheel and I checked out Halsey. He was still out cold, but he had a pulse. When we got to Wythetown, we went directly to the police station.

Rollie was on duty. He called the rescue squad for Halsey as I gave him information about Sid. I had just begun telling my story when a call came in about shots being fired at a farm. A few minutes later, a motorist reported gunshots. Immediately Rollie had the entire police force on the way as well as the state police.

By the time the Police Chief Thompson got to the station, Rollie was tracking the calls with pushpins on a large county map. Sid was heading toward Wythetown. It not every day that a small town police department has a drugged up, homicidal maniac on its hands. For people use to writing parking tickets and drunk and disorderly arrests, this was a dream come true. They could show their metal. Thompson was impressive and decisive. I had been wrong about him.

The calls stopped for about a half an hour and then there was a call from a secluded cabin. Someone had been shot there. It was one in the morning, but every light in Wythetown was on. Policemen and Sheriff's Deputies were everywhere. State Trooper's cruisers began to arrive. I went out of the station to get some fresh air. There were flashing lights and sirens everywhere. By the sirens had stopped. Several State Police copters were waiting for morning, as were K-9 teams from all over the state. At dawn, they would be ready.

I would guess 70% of the town's residents were hunters, so there was no shortage of arms. I was more worried about people shooting their neighbors, than getting Sid. The local radios stations set up a remote broadcast from the Police station. Chief Thompson and the Town Manager, woman named Elisabeth Rollins, were calm and helpful.

Three EMTs worked on Halsey, but they couldn't get him to wake up. There was a huge gash in his head and one of his fingers almost had been cut off. There was a med-evac copter on the way. The local doctor thought Halsey's non-responsiveness might be due to blood loss, rather than a cranial fracture. It had been dark and we hadn't realized how much he was bleeding. The four of us looked like something out of a grade B horror movie. We were covered in blood.

I was going to take the police to the campsite, but Thompson wouldn't allow that until day light. "Too much opportunity for an ambush," he said.

Sean went with Halsey on the copter to the University Hospital. I saw the diner had opened. I went with Juan and Reggie to see Andy. Some coffee would be good, but a shower would be better. We were lucky Andy was there. The Troopers, deputies and cops at the diner didn't think well of three, blood-covered rednecks. Andy vouched for us. Once that was straight, all was well. I got to shower. It was hard to get the dried blood off. Andy had an herbal body wash that worked well. Andy gave one of his tee shirts to replace my blood soaked one. It was one of those spaghetti strapped things. Since Andy was twice my size, I was all but shirtless.

When I was cleaned up, I returned to the diner for some food. Most of the men and women at the diner were K-9 tracking units. I gave them detailed descriptions of Sid. They appreciated that. Trooper Fluffy loved me. Fluffy was big tan dog with brown eyes.

Fluffy's partner, a big trooper who looked like Bluto was impressed. "Fluffy must think you're a relative," he joked. "Damn, you're a hair ball." I looked at my chest. The body wash had fluffed up my chest and shoulder hair. It looked as if I had a halo of two or three inches of hair surrounding my body.

"Damn, it looks as if I've had it teased," I said.

"I'd sure love to see what Queer Eye for the Straight guy could do with you," another trooper said. He was a blond, crew cut type.

"I'm not sure your taste for fishnet tank tops is just right for you," the man who looked like Bluto said, imitating one of the queer guys. Our eyes met. He looked away quickly. I noticed something about him I guessed he didn't know himself.

The sun was coming up. I went back to the police station. They had cancelled school and the town had begun to look like an armed camp. There had been no shots since 2:30 that morning. I went with Bluto, Fluffy and the crew cut blond to our camp. Bluto's real name was Robert Delance and his partner was Frank. I had called Robert Bluto and he liked it. A second K-9 crew came with us. The other ones went to the places where shots were fired.

Frank gave Fluffy a sniff of Sid's clothes and Fluffy went crazy. "Is she a drug sniffer too?" I asked.

"You got it," Bluto said. "Fetch!" he commanded. Fluffy went right to Sid's backpack. Good dog!" Bluto said it was crack cocaine. Sid's car hadn't been moved, so he was on foot. Another team of troopers would watch it in case he circled back to make his getaway.

Fluffy was very excited and ready to go. "I guess he doesn't want to stay back," I said.

"That's the way it looks to me," Bluto said. "Are you ready to do some tracking, Fluffy?" Of course, the dog said yes. "How about you, Clydesdale?"

"Sure, it's nice day for a walk in the woods," I said. I went to my tent and got some bug repellant. I sprayed the troopers and me before we set off. After a half hour, we came by a campsite. It had been trashed and the tent cut up, but there was no blood. Whoever had been there either was with Sid, or had escaped. Bluto called for more back up. We found a clearing nearby and had them send in copters. Ten minutes later, a search and rescue team arrived. They would look for the campers as we continued looking for Sid. Frank stayed at the camp to aid the second K-9 team that was on the way.

Part 10

If I had an ounce of common sense, I would have rested until more reinforcements came. I'm afraid Bluto, Fluffy and I are all Alpha male types. We charged ahead. Fluffy was on the trail and had no desire to stop. It would be nice if we could catch Sid and do a little pre sentencing punishment before he went to court.

There were only two of us, but with the dog, I figured we were effectively four. Fluffy could smell and hear. We had gone another half mile into the woods when Fluffy stopped dead in his tracks.

"What is it big guy?" Bluto asked. Fluffy began moving slowly off to the side.

"He smells something," Bluto whispered.

"Sid?"

"No, it must be something else. He much more aggressive when he finds the perpetrator," Bluto explained. Fluffy moved slowly through the underbrush. Bluto may have thought it wasn't Sid, but he had his gun out anyway. Fluffy stopped, the circled a tree. I looked up and saw a small foot dangling from a branch. I motioned to Bluto and got him to look up.

"It's all right. We're the Police," he said in a firm voice. A small face looked out from the branches. "You're safe with us," he said.

"Have they caught the guy yet?" the boy asked.

"Not yet, but half the county is after him," I said. The boy came down. His clothes were torn, but he looked all right.

"Where's Dad?" he asked.

"We don't know yet," he said. "He was with you?"

"We were camping," the boy said. "This crazy man came at us. Dad told us to run. He'd decoy the guy away from us." Bluto pulled out his radio and called in the information.

"What does your Dad look like?" Bluto asked. The boy gave a brief description.

"Name?"

"Richard Williamson," the boy replied.

"Are you from Mt. Holly?"

"Yes sir," the boy answered.

"I went to high school with your dad," Bluto said. "Did he ever mention Bobby Delance to you?"

"Crazy Bobby?"

"That's me," Bluto replied.

The boy laughed. "Charlie, you can come out now. It's okay," he called. Another boy dropped out of the tree. He was younger than his brother. He was almost crying.

"Is Daddy okay?"

"I'm sure he is," Bluto said reassuringly. "He knows how to take care of himself." Fluffy was at attention again. A few seconds later, we heard something moving toward us. Bluto pulled out his gun again.

"Boys, you come with me," I whispered. "We'll hide." We went to the rear of the big tree and disappeared into a thicket. The sounds got closer. Fluffy was very alert but not showing signs of aggression. I hoped it wasn't Sid. I wanted to get the man, but not under manned and with two children to protect.

"Halt. This is the police!" Bluto said in his most assertive voice.

"Thank God," another voice replied.

"Daddy!" Charlie cried. They raced out to greet their father. There were two reunions, one with the kids and their dad and the other between Crazy Bobby and Dickie. Dickie looked bad, he was beaten up and really dirty, but he was happy.

Bluto called in the information on the kids. We began to return to the campsite where we could turn over Dickie and his sons to the State Police. You don't want to save a family then lose them again if Sid came back. It took most of the afternoon to get back.

The campsite was swarming with Police, Deputies and Troopers. Sid was still at large. There was no sign of him. He was lying low or in hiding. He had shot two other persons, but only one was badly hurt. I was hot to trot and wanted to get back on the trail, but Fluffy sat down and fell asleep. I had been up for 24 hours and I figured I probably needed some rest.

The boys' mother arrived with her parents. She and Dickie were separated or divorced. They took the kids away. Dickie offered to take us home and let us crash there. Bluto took him to an old logging trail where Dickie had parked his truck. Then Dickie led us to his house. He lived in an old hunting cabin about ten miles away. He had an old Lab named Sally who hit it off with Fluffy right away. As Bobby and Dickie talked, it was clear Dickie had fallen on bad times, but I got the feeling he would pull out of it.

Dickie grilled steaks and cooked fries. It was a good straightforward meal. I sat on the sofa as they talked and woke up at about five the next morning. I had slept nine hours without moving. I hate to think of myself as getting old, but I have never been so stiff in my life. I could barely move.

I went to the bathroom, took a leak and then got in the shower. I figured a long, hot shower might loosen me up some. I was in the shower for less than a minute when I heard someone pissing. The cabin had only one bath.

Bluto's face peeked in. "Don't use up all the hot water," he said.

"I'll be careful," I said. I was in the water for another minute, then turned it off and opened the curtain. Bluto was still there. I dried off slowly. "It's all yours."

"Take your time, I'm in no rush," he said. He was looking me over.

"I'd hate to blow my own horn, but for some reason, guys seem to find me more interesting with my clothes off than on," I said.

Bluto laughed a little. "Why is that?" He was staring at my cock.

The door opened and Dickie came in. "What's this, a convention?" he asked. He saw me naked and then he saw my cock. "Shit, is that fucker real?" We all laughed. I'm pretty sure he was thinking out loud.

"It's real," I said. "It seems to be an attention grabber." I was drying my cock, so I peeled back the skin and exposed my cock head.

"So that's why they call you Clydesdale?" Bluto said. "Your mother got fucked by a horse?"

I nodded. "The kids in school called me that. They thought it was an insult," I explained, "The Coach thought it was a compliment, so it stuck. I'd rather be called horse cocked than mosquito cocked." Bluto was naked, and Dickie was only wearing a robe. Bluto was huge and muscular. His cock looked small in comparison to his body. It was firming up some, but Dickie's cock was poking out from his robe. It was hard as a rock.

"That's a lot of cock," Bluto said. "It's enough for two men."

"I've been known to share," I said. "I'm a New Testament kind of guy. Do unto other, as you would have them do unto you. Do you get my drift?" It was a small bath, so I reached out and fondled both their balls. Bluto immediately dropped to his knees and began sucking me.

"Are you guys' old friends?" I asked, "Playmates?"

"We messed around some when we were kids," Dickie said. "We kind of had a good time last night after you fell asleep. Do you mess around?"

"Only when I get the opportunity," I said. "Somehow, when I get naked, the opportunity arises." Dickie smiled.

We went to the bedroom, but it was hard to get Bluto off my cock. It had worked its magic again. It's a gay man magnet. We got in a three-man daisy chain. I sucked Dickie, as he sucked Bluto and Bluto did me. Dickie was average sized, but he possessed a genuine joystick. Everything you licked, sucked, or touched on his cock caused a reaction. I worked a finger toward his ass and he didn't object. I guessed Dickie could be full service if he was inspired.

"It's my turn to try that monster," Dickie said. Reluctantly Bluto gave up his Hoover like connection to my cock and we traded partners. Fully erect, Bluto had a seven-inch probe with a big knob. It curved and almost formed a "C." Bluto was a massive man, but his cock seemed delicate in comparison to his body. I had expected a fireplug style member.

While Dickie was a moaner and very responsive, Bluto was less demonstrative. He was, however, cock crazed, sucking on Dickey's cock like a starved newborn on his mother's breast, but nothing I did to his cock seemed to cause any reaction. He had a big ball sack that seemed barely able to hold his monster balls. Dickie possessed low hanging eggs. Bluto had high and tight apples.

I hate to sound as if I had made a detailed study of men's genitals, but I got the impression Bluto's equipment had been assembled by a committee and was made of leftover parts. I was licking his balls and as my tongue got closer to his hole, he got excited.

Licking a finger, I touched his ass hole. It was as if I had said, "Abracadabra, open sesame." I had found the magic button that opened him up.

"Can we take a breather," Dickie asked, "I need to take a piss." We broke apart as he went to the bathroom.

"Do you think you can take it?" I asked. "You muscle men have trouble opening up sometimes." I pushed my finger deeper into his ass to inspire him.

"I'd love to try," Bluto said. He looked around the room. "Do you think we could do it without Dickie?" I must have looked puzzled. "He doesn't know I bottom," Bluto explained. Reading between the lines, I knew Bluto topped and had topped Dickie.

"I'm not the shy type," I said. "You need to decide if you want to remain a top or get fucked to the moon."

"Who's going to get fucked?" Dickie said as he re entered the room.

"I was trying to talk your friend here into taking a chance," I said. "I hadn't got to the point of explaining it would be best if you were to open him up. I would go in for sloppy seconds."

"Would it fit?" Dickie asked. "It's huge."

"I've given anal CPR several times," I said. "You either love it, or it just doesn't fit."

"Do you want to try it?" Dickie asked of Bluto. Bluto looked uncertain, but then he nodded.

"Do you have some lube?" I asked. Dickie went to the bath and returned with a tube of K-Y and a bottle of lotion. He coated his cock with it and I did Bluto's ass. I straddled Bluto's face and held his legs wide and high. He was a muscular man and I wanted him open. I was a little worried he'd object to having my balls and ass hole in his face. When he started to tongue my ass, I knew it wasn't a problem.

Dickie was in position, but holding back. "Just pop it in," I said. Dickie was a bit timid. He stepped up to the plate and pushed. Nothing happened. "Don't be shy, push harder. He can take it." Dickie pushed and his entire cock vanished into Bluto's ass.

Bluto tensed, then relaxed. I leaned forward and sucked Bluto's cock as Dickie took long strokes. I had Bluto's legs held back, so I had both a front line seat watching the fucking. I tasted him react. When I sucked Bluto before there was no precum, but now it was flowing in a steady stream.

Dickie had a nice cock, but when he pulled all the way out to give Bluto a deep poke, I noticed it was larger and more bloated than it had been earlier when I sucked him. Bluto had a hairy ass. The hairs stuck to Dickie's cock as he pulled out forming a collar of hair. When Dickie pushed, the hair and the cock vanished into the quivering ass.

"I can't last much longer," Dickie said.

"Shoot it as deep as you can," I said. "He's going to need it really deep when I poke him." Dickie's entire body began to twitch as he rear loaded Bluto. He pulled out. I'm a fast mover when there's an empty ass quivering in anticipation. I coated my cock and pushed it into the recently vacated hole.

Dickie was on the bed still shivering from his climax. His cock was still spurting. I pushed.

"Jesus!" Bluto exclaimed. "Can you take it slow?"

"No problem," I said. "You can change your mind anytime if it's too much. I'm trying to fuck your ass, not tear you a new one." I was sure he could take it, but giving him an out would make him more comfortable. I'm not a believer in the no pain, no gain school of sex. I like sex without collateral damage.

I took my time. Dickie rallied and helped out. I didn't know how much Dickie was into man sex. Some guys just take what they can get. He was divorced and he might be on the rebound. Poor Bluto had taken as much as he could, when Dickie produced an unopened bottle of Jungle Juice. Dickie was a dues paying member of the Fraternity. He had Bluto take a snort and he opened up wide. My cock went into the hilt.

Once I was in, we rested. "Damn," Bluto said.

"If I had another inch or two, I'd shove it in you, but you've taken all I have," I said. "Are you okay?"

"I guess so," he said. I pulled out an inch or inch and a half and then shoved it in again. His eyes rolled back in his head and he pulled his legs closer to his chest. That was a good sign. His cock had been at half-staff. I gave his ass a few more short thrusts and it re inflated.

Dickie gave Bluto another snort of the Jungle Juice, and then I took one. I pulled out further then pushed in deeper. Bluto had no problem with that, so we went with it. It was good, but not perfect. I sensed I was missing something. I pulled out, flipped him over and screwed him doggy style. Poor Bluto didn't know what hit him.

I don't think anyone had used his prostate as a cock punching bag before. I shoved deep. Bluto would growl, and then I'd do it again. After a while, he'd beg me to stop because he couldn't take it anymore. I'd pull out and a few seconds he'd beg me to fuck him again.

Normally a guy will loosen up after he's been screwed for a while, but Bluto had buns of steel. I'd pull out and his ass would close up just as tight as it had been for my first penetration. I'd force my cock through his sphincter. Once my head was in, the shaft followed easily. His sphincter would tighten again, grabbing my shaft.

I don't know how long we did it, but he finally collapsed on the bed. I rolled him over. He was still rock hard, so I straddled him and sat on his cock. His cock was curved and when as it slipped in my ass it made a direct hit on my prostate. I had been hoping for a leisurely ride on his joystick, but my cock exploded like a Roman candle. Dickie had the odd habit of counting the individual cum spurts. He counted to 23 before they merged into a general sperm drool.

"Damn!" Dickie said. I felt the earth shake. It was Bluto, ejaculating into my ass. He was one of those men who have whole body ejaculations. Dickie counted to ten. Bluto was asleep by eleven. The morning was off to a good start.

Part II

The next day we were back on the trail. Sid had vanished. He hadn't struck me as much of a woodsman, but he was well hidden in the forest. It was time for Fluffy to do his work. This time we were with a full team, well equipped and well armed. I had called into my office and with Sid's name, soon alarm bells were going off up and down the east coast. He was a small time con man who had been associated with several scams.

Sid was a spear-carrier, not a leader of men. He also had a problem with women. Sid liked hurting them and he liked knives. My office was checking into this. Apparently, my Aunt was the first time he got to play with knives big time. This made me sick. He liked cutting up women. Edith was already dead when he cut her. I was afraid the next one wouldn't be. The State Troopers felt the same way.

I figured things would be alright in Wythetown itself. By now, the Police chief had all but fortified the town. I was more worried about isolated farms, or cabins. There were people in the woods who didn't do news.

Some were mountain folks who were living in another century. They were sitting ducks.

It was a race between Sid and the cops. Sid might be hopped up on drugs. We only had adrenaline, but we had a lot of it. Fluffy, the police dog, Bluto, two cops from the county and I set off at dawn. Fluffy found the smell immediately and was on the trace. This time we were well equipped and had good communications.

Fluffy and I saw eye to eye about things. You can't trick a dog. Being cute, or wealthy or well connected doesn't cut it with a dog. You treat them well and you're a friend for life. If you treat them badly, you're up shit creek. Dogs are good judges of character too. They can tell something is off about a guy in seconds. A quick sniff of the ass is all they need to know all they need to know.

Dogs have always liked me. My Mom said it was because they thought I was a distant relative. I don't sniff asses much, but I've sure been known to get to know a guy really well by sucking his cock.

Fluffy had only smelled Sid, but they were already sworn enemies. Saving the boys and their father was good, but Fluffy wanted to catch the bad guy. He was a tracker. He wanted Sid. I wanted the same.

The search for Sid was well organized by now. The area had been subdivided into quadrants and teams assigned to each. We were on the trail when we got a call from Chief Thompson. "The GPS says you're near a cabin owned by Stanford Mills. He's a survivalist guy," Thompson said. "You know, the Commies are coming, repent of all your sins, the end is near type. He's got daughters, real pretty daughters."

Thompson gave us the cabin's GPS coordinates. We were off. I was worried we'd disappoint Fluffy again, but Fluffy seemed pleased as punch. That was a bad sign. I didn't like that at all. He smelled something. We moved at a brisk pace. As we got closer to the camp, Fluffy got excited and started to pull.

Bluto called headquarters. "The dog's going bonkers," he said. "Fluffy's found something fresh, I think. Send backup."

As we got closer, I smelled smoke. It was the acrid smell I associate with a house fire. Bluto called in again and warned HQ about a fire. We were all running now. I could see the cabin. It was burning, but not fully involved yet. Bluto and the dog ran past the cabin into the woods. I went to the cabin.

"Is anyone in here?" I screamed. The ceiling was hidden by smoke, but I could still see the floor. I guessed the fire had just been started.

"Save the girls!" a weak voice cried. "They're in the back room." I ran to an open door. Two small girls were tied with duct tape to chairs. One girl was young, maybe five or six. The other was 14 or so. I grabbed the chairs and dragged them outside. A copter landed in a clearing next to the house. Two policemen and a policewoman ran over to us and took the girls. I ran back into the cabin. By now, the smoke was three or four feet from the floor.

"Where are you?" I called. I heard a moan from the right. "The girls are safe." It took a while, but I found him.

"I'm cut bad," he whispered.

"This may hurt, but it's better than burning," I said as I grabbed him. He was a big man and almost too much for me. The smoke was hanging low in the room and I could see flames. I got almost to the door before I passed out.

Thank you Jesus for the volunteer firemen. They got us both out.

When I woke up a while later, we were back at the headquarters. I found out the guy I had pulled out was Stanford Mills. He was in bad shape and had been taken by the copter to Roanoke. The two girls weren't hurt, but they were terrorized. A woman EMT was with them. Apparently, Sid liked the idea of burning the girls and their Dad alive. It was clear Sid had gone way off the deep end. I want to go after him, but the EMTs wouldn't let me go. I didn't know what they were worried about.

The police had several trailers they used for communications. One had a shower in it. The EMTs told me to use it. In the bathroom, they had a mirror. I was shocked when I saw myself. I was covered in soot and my beard was a lot shorter. Part had burned off. I had no idea how close to getting cooked I had been.

When I took a shower, the hot water hurt. I tried all cold water and it felt good. When I got out, I looked like a lobster. My hands really hurt. I began to cough and soot came up. My lungs were filled with soot.

When the EMTs saw me they were concerned and decided I should go to the hospital. By then I felt so bad I didn't fight it at all. I heard them muttering something about shock. They took me off in an ambulance. I spent the night the night getting oxygen and with an IV in my arm. I felt a little better the next day. My hands were wrapped in bandages. They hurt like hell.

I had a TV set in the room and saw the local news. There were detailed descriptions of the capture. Fluffy was the hero of the day. He got his man. Sid had been cornered. He had third girl with him. Sid had a knife to the girl's throat. Unfortunately, for Sid police dog training often features a man with a knife. Sid's knife was like a piece of raw meat in front of a starving tiger. Fluffy knew his duty. Apparently, Sid never saw the dog. The girl escaped at the first bite.

Sadly, Bluto got Fluffy off of Sid before he had a chance to do serious damage. Sid was alive and being interrogated. I guessed he would spill the beans. He was so far up shit creek he had to do anything that would spare him from lethal injection. I noted they sent him to jail in Roanoke. The police were worried about the local reaction in Wytheville.

As the special report on the TV came to an end, the Doctor came and told me what was up. My hands were burned, but not badly. "It's just surface burns, but they will hurt like hell for a few days," he said. "You need to be careful about infections." They were afraid I was slipping into shock the day before, but I was better now, except for my hands. I could go home, but I'd have to come in each day to change the dressings on my hands.

I was trying to figure out what to do when Rev. Pettigrew and Tom Robinson dropped by. Rev. Pettigrew was on his normal round of hospital visits. "Stay at the Rectory," Tom suggested. "There's tons of room and I've got a lot of spare time."

Pettigrew smiled. "Tom's organist position is endowed," he explained. "He has to play on Sunday and the rest is up to him." Tom was in the rescue squad too and was a certified EMT, so he could handle the burns. I went off to the rectory. Both Tom and Rev. Pettigrew had been playmates, so I assumed there would be some fun at the rectory.

Once and a while you discover a real advantage to be gay and a cock hound, this was one of those times. I couldn't use my hands, but I had friends. I wasn't shy about my cock and my friends had no problem helping me take a piss. In fact, they seemed to like aiming it. Showering was good too. There was no shortage in volunteers. Andy and Festus from the diner as well as Rollie and Scooter were all willing to help.

It's fair to say my friends had a warm spot for me and an even warmer spot for my cock. Every time I needed to take a piss, I needed someone to aim. Since I'm uncut, I have to peel the skin back to insure a clear shot. I am afraid my friends took my misfortune as an excuse to play with my member. There was no shortage of pals who wanted to help me peel and piss.

I had never tried a steady diet of hands free sex before, but I was willing. Having your hand available for a quick boost as you get down to the final push toward an orgasm was normal. A climax is an involuntary action once it gets going. It was odd not to be able to touch my cock, or even scratch my balls. As it turned out my hands free interlude was good, except for my hands of course.

My first night at the house was the worst. I had pain pills, but they wore off at an inopportune time. Tom thought it would be best if I slept nude. That made it easier for me to get to the toilet. He was in the next room, but it was 3:00 PM when the pill wore off and I really needed another. I woke him up. He gave me the pill and held the glass of water. He didn't have any straws, but he got them the next day. He got into bed with me.

The pain pill took effect at about 7:00, so it wasn't a good night. One of Tom's choir members, Dan, arrived at breakfast in time to help. Dan lived above the Rectory's garage and worked at a lumberyard. He was a bass in the choir and looked a little bit like Lurch in the Addams Family. Dan was 6'-6" tall and must have been nearly 300 pounds of mostly muscle. He was slow moving and deliberate in all his movements. I hadn't seen him around.

Dan was slow. He had a beautiful voice and natural musical sense according to Tom. He was gainfully employed. Tom and his fellow choir members liked Dan. They both helped and protected him. He had been in a bad job where his boss took advantage of him. Tom got him a job at the lumberyard owned by the best tenor in the choir.

When Dan saw my cock for the first time, I saw his face light up. Dan was a pure, unadulterated size queen. Seeing my cock was like a trip to the Louvre for an art lover. He loved it. I hate the idea of taking advantage of a person with limitations, but Dan had his own interests and I didn't mind helping him have some fun. I think Dan thought of me as a toy, as a delicate toy. On Sunday, Tom and Pettigrew were busy, and I spent the morning with Dan. He helped me take a shower. He liked being naked with me.

He was massive, but his cock was a long, thin, seven incher topped with a bulbous head. He got hard as soon as he started washing me. He made sure my cock and asshole were really clean, so I was hard too. It didn't take long for me to realize that while he loved my cock, my ass ran a close second. As he sucked my cock, he worked a thick, long finger into my ass. He went straight for my prostate and pressed it as he sucked.

It was good, but I was holding my arms up to keep the bandages from getting wet. That was a problem and I got tired. I told Dan I was tired, so he turned the water off and dried me off.

"My hands felt better when they were up, but my arms get tired," I said.

"I can help you," Dan said. He sat on a chair. "Sit on my lap," he said. I sat, but he told me to sit facing him. "Sit on my cock," he explained. The pain pills worked but they made me feel dopey. I figured why not. His meat was already covered in precum. Dan was excited.

His cock slid into my ass easily. Dan put his arms around me. "Put your arms on my shoulders," he said. He was so much bigger than me my hands were elevated and my arms relaxed. I was comfortable for the first time in days.

I thought this arrangement would be uncomfortable for Dan, but my weight was nothing to him. His cock stayed hard so there was no danger I would slip off. He didn't exactly fuck me. He just tensed his ass so his cock made small movements in my ass. This kept him hard and got me hard too.

The painkillers, my elevated hands and the anal stimulation let me relax and I fell asleep. I woke an hour later, feeling a lot better.

"I'd better move," I said. "You must be exhausted."

"I'm fine," Dan said. "I shot off in your ass. I hope you aren't mad at me?"

I smiled. "No problem, it's the least I could do."

Dan looked relieved. "It did it three times."

"Three times is better," I said. "You're still hard."

"I like you," he said. "You're nice."

I got off his cock and we took another shower. I was presentable in time for lunch with Festus and Andy from the diner. Festus and Dan were pals. Andy had invited Rollie and Scooter over so we traded information. Andy brought a great lunch for us and we washed it down with wine. They took turns helping me eat. We were finishing up when Bluto and came by with the latest news. He stopped in at the Rectory and found out I was at Andy's.

Sid was singing like a bird. There was a double scam. He was doing some espionage on competitors. The legitimate exploration companies did the work and he would try to steal the property before they had a chance to file.

Sid was also a spear-carrier for a Mafia family. Apparently, they kept him under tight rein given his sadistic tendencies. They didn't want him freelancing. Apparently, they thought a nice, small rural county in Virginia might be a good place to set up shop. He was to buy land and they would move in. They didn't think the coal thing was going to work out, but it would be a good way to launder money. An unsuccessful mine would swallow up cash without a trace.

Aunt Edith was the fly in the ointment. She didn't trust anyone, not to mention a low life character like Sid. Her land holdings were so extensive that by purchasing her properties the Mafia's needs could be accomplished in short order. Sid wanted to prove his worth his bosses. When Edith balked, Sid got carried away.

I think if Sid had just killed her, he might have gotten away with it. After killing her, Sid took a few hits of his favorite mood enhancer, crack cocaine, and then he cut her up. When he returned to earth, he knew the dismembered body was a problem, so he set the fire. Apparently, he thought this would destroy the body. It takes one hell of fire to totally destroy a corpse, but Sid wasn't thinking too clearly.

I found myself drifting off to sleep. The painkiller's had their effect. Andy took me back to the Rectory bedroom and I slept for the rest of the afternoon. I woke up for a little while and then fell asleep again. Sometimes you don't know how tired you are. I had been on the go at full speed for weeks and it all caught up with me.

I woke up at five in the morning, took a leak by myself then got back to bed with Tom. Tom woke up and snuggled up to me. I got hard as a rock. Tom had some lubricant by the bed. He coated my cock with it and we slow fucked. Tom was much more relaxed than he had been before and the penetration was easy. There was a little resistance at his sphincter, but my organ slid in effortlessly. Effortless is not the same as ineffective. Tom shivered and twitched as I probed deep. I must have accidentally tripped every sexual switch in Tom's body.

I got turned on big time as he responded. His excitement was contagious. It was a long session. I pushed him up to the edge of a climax and then let him down. I did this three or four times, but with each session, my cock got tenderer and I got closer to shooting. Fucking with your meat cocked and with a hair trigger is a trip.

Dan joined us and sucked Tom as I fucked the organist. It took me ten or twelve seconds to realize Dan was a sperm hound. Tom couldn't have held off shooting as Dan sucked his load. My cock was still in Tom's ass and I felt him twitch as he ejaculated. I pulled out after he shot off. He was one of those guys who gets hyper sensitive after an orgasm.

Dan got up and smiled at me. His mouth was filled with Tom's cum. He looked at my cock. I was on my back. He squirted some lube on his hand and then greased up his ass.

"Dan, you've never taken a cock like Clydesdale's," Tom murmured. "Are you sure you want to try it?" Dan nodded as he straddled me. He held my cock and guided it to his hole.

"You're a lot bigger than Clydesdale," Tom said. "Don't hurt him." Then Dan sat back on my cock. Dan skewered himself on my meat with the delicacy of a ballerina on the stage. He had incredible muscle control. All his weight was on his legs and massive thighs. I provided only the tool. Dan fucked himself. He did a little hula dance, rotating his hips in a corkscrew manner, working my cock into his rectum.

His bloated cock deflated when my cock head popped his sphincter. I hate hurting a guy and I was worried my cock was too much. A few inches later, all was well. He was rock hard again and drooling precum.

Dan had most of it in when I began to pulse my hips. Dan moaned. "Do that again!" he cried. I did. All of his 300 pounds was precariously balanced on my cock. I pumped a few times and he began to shoot. Dan must have lost a quarter of his weight as he ejaculated. I didn't know a guy could have that much cum in his balls. As he shot, his entire rectum contracted pushing me over the edge.

Remarkably, he kept his balance as he climaxed. It was a spectacular performance.

We all showered and then went to breakfast. I had plans for more fun, but that wasn't to be. Elizabeth, Scooter's mom had called my mother. Mom and my Aunts had gone on a vacation to recover from the ordeal of Edith's death. I thought there was no way to contact them. That was good because I didn't want to worry them.

I hadn't counted on the respectable Presbyterian Ladies Emergency Telegraph. Elizabeth found her. They came to Wytheville, and carried me off to Mom's house that afternoon. I had a strictly enforced week of recovery and rest in my old bedroom. Mom is a nurse, firm, but fair. It was unbelievably boring, and surprisingly enjoyable.

My hands were healed in a week and Donnan wanted me back to fill in gaps in the story. I was also need to clear up the status of Reggie, Sean, Halsey and Juan. Sid had generously been trying to spread the blame. Reggie and Juan were in the county lock up. Halsey had just gotten out of the hospital. His brain injury had been serious. Sean was free since he was obviously too dumb to know anything.

Halsey knew more about the operation than the other men. He had seen Sid torching my Aunt's house, but was too scared to turn Sid in. Halsey was smart and knew he was in trouble. I talked with Chief Thompson. I offered to question Halsey and get the info, but I'd like to help Halsey out.

We had a little talk and Thompson volunteered that having your head split open could be exchanged for jail time. "To tell you the truth Halsey's medical problems could cost the county a lot of money. Jail won't help that at all. I'm not too sure he'd survive it. Can you get him to talk?"

"I think so."

"Can I take him away from here?" I asked. "The jail has too many bad vibes."

"In your custody?" Thompson asked,

"Sure, I'll take responsibility," I replied. I called Tom, my organist friend and asked if he could help me out. He said yes. They brought Halsey to me from the jail. He looked awful, weak and pale. I could see why they didn't want him in the jail. He looked fragile. He almost cried when I said I was taking him to the rectory.

I took him to the bedroom. He sat on the bed and fell asleep sitting up. We got him into bed and covered him up. He slept for six hours. He was wiped out. Rev. Pettigrew sat with him. When I went to look in on him later in the day, they were talking quietly. Pettigrew was wearing his clerical collar and a cross and a minister was just what Halsey needed. Pettigrew wasn't a fire and brimstone preacher man; he was calm and reassuring. He wanted Halsey to confess his sins and get right with God and his fellowmen. Pettigrew was a calm and reassuring man, and Halsey responded.

"I need to speak with Halsey," I said.

"Certainly," Rev. Pettigrew responded, "Could you give me a little while longer? I'd like to finish my conversation." I nodded and went in thirty minutes later. Halsey looked better and was calm.

"How far up the creek am I?" he asked.

"It's not good, but it could be worse," I said, "I made a deal with the Police Chief. If you do what I tell you to do you won't go to jail."

He looked at me as if I were Jesus come back to earth. "Really?" he said and then began to cry. When he pulled himself back together he said, "I thought I was a goner."

I told him to give me the full story. I needed every detail. I took notes. His information was good. I was afraid the combination of alcoholism and a skull fracture would be bad. The story began a bit confused, but as he went on it became clearer. He went back to the beginning and corrected inconsistencies and confusing items.

He also remembered names and addresses. He was an engineer and remembered the phone numbers at the headquarters of the fake exploration company. I called Thompson and gave him the information. Halsey and I had dinner with Will. Will was a good cook and it was a success. The next morning Halsey looked like a new man.

Thompson sent over a court reporter to take Halsey's statement. Halsey presented it as an organized report. He had a good memory, especially for numbers and names. Oddly, Halsey didn't know who these people were. They were just names mentioned by his boss or friends of his boss. When Thompson ran them through the police computer bells started to go off from Richmond to Washington and into Dallas. The computer knew who they were. Most names seemed to be associated with organized crime. They weren't the big time men, but they were involved. There was one person Halsey referred to as his Lordship. He was elusive. Sid denied he ever used the term, but Halsey remembered it clearly.

Oddly, Aunt Edith's murder became a positive asset in the investigation. It was essentially a shakedown by petty crooks trying to swindle a larger corporation. The phrase, "a possible accessory to murder" was all but magic. There was a virtual stampede of men trying to turn in their business associates. Most were successful.

Sean appeared at the door to see Halsey. Reggie and Juan were in jail, just in case they knew something. I told Thompson they didn't and so I got them out. Chief Thompson wanted them to stay around and told them they could stay at his cabin. He had some odd jobs that needed to be done, so he offered them a short time job.

I think Chief Thompson had finely tuned Gaydar and he had sniffed potential for some fun. When Juan entered the room, I saw a glint in his eye. I think he had a taste for younger men. I thought he didn't like Mexicans, but apparently he was willing to make exceptions.

Thompson told me Sid had confessed to killing Aunt Edith, but said it was a spur of thing. He had been aggravated and struck her with a heavy glass vase. Sid said he was shaken when he found out she was dead and dipped into the Crystal Meth to get some courage. The dismemberment was drug induced recreational interlude. Sid said he got a bad batch and that was the reason for the rampage later on.

All of this would result in one hell of a prison sentence, but no death penalty. He figured that much out. He wouldn't give any information about his Lordship. However, he was willing to sacrifice everyone else. Aunt Edith's murder was resolved. There still was a problem with land ownership in rural Virginia.

Part 12

It was a week later I was back in Richmond when my computer guys found something interesting. Denny was a retired cop who had lost a leg to diabetes. He stayed home all day and cruised the internet. He discovered Resource Management was registered as a corporation in Virginia. Of course, all corporations need to be registered in Virginia, but given the fly by night nature of Resource Management, I had assumed they skipped that nicety.

Mark Jones, the guy I had met at the motel had vanished and hadn't been using his real name anyway. The corporate officers had vanished too. They had been peons in Texas law firms. The only officer they found was a black lady named Ruby Morris. She was the janitor and thought she had been witnessing a will when she signed a corporate document.

The contact for Resource Management in Virginia was none other than Byron Q. R. Semple, Edith's lawyer. He had been kind enough to offer to buy all of Edith's properties when he met my Mom and Aunts at Elizabeth and Scooter's house.

I called Chief Thompson and gave him that information.

"Well, isn't that a bit of a shock!" he exclaimed. "He didn't exactly volunteer that information when your Aunt died did he?"

"He didn't mention it during the hunt for Sid either," I added. "What sort of a lawyer is he?"

"Byron is a strange case. His mom's daddy, Quinton Randall, was a distinguished lawyer who eventually became a judge. His mom married Byron Semple who was a nice guy but nothing else. Byron took over his granddad's office and inherited his clients. I think Byron's smart enough, but he's lazy. He never had any desire to work hard since he had a client list of old families. Wills and deeds provide an adequate income. There has been a little suspicion of some irregularities in trusts and a few problems where he was the executor of estates. Byron talked his way out of the problem.

"I think I may take a trip to visit you," I said. "Mom and my Aunts are thinking about repairing the house for sale. By the way, you might check on some of Mr. Semple's estates. Have there been some fire sales?"

"I'll do that," Thompson said, "This new information puts a new light on things. I hope you'll have some time to renew old acquaints. You have been missed."

Semple was the trustee of Edith's estate and my Mom and Aunts were the co-executors. I called Mom and told her what was up.

"I'm glad you called," she said. "Graham and his son have been helping me. They haven't exactly made friends with Byron. His record keeping isn't up to snuff. Carl seems to have made friends with the county clerk, Jonathan. Jonathan seems quite disturbed at some things that have been going on."

"You might suggest to Carl that he call Chief Thompson. There is a chance Byron is in way over his head. If he catches wind of trouble, it could be bad."

"Cornered rats are dangerous?" Mom said.

"That's a possibility," I replied. Wythetown is a small place. News travels fast." Mom was a good nurse and she was good at noticing the danger signs well before actual symptoms appeared. She never ignored early warnings. I called Scooter and asked if I could use the doublewide as a crash pad. He was more than willing.

I drove into Wythetown and met with Jonathan and Carl. The three of us went to visit Police Chief Thompson. Jonathan and Carl actually did not accuse Byron of any wrongdoing. They simply organized information about some recent sales and made sense of it. Byron Sample had been buying properties for a decade and the pace had picked up recently. Many of the purchases were related to estates. Jonathan crosschecked the purchases with the date of death of the seller. They normally occurred two weeks after the death. Earlier purchases were 15% below market rate, but the more recent ones were 17.5% below assessed valuations.

Jonathan explained there was an informal rule that sales of 20% less than the assessed valuation would be noted and sent to the Probate court. All of Byron's sales were below that number. Carl had found some sales from estates to relatives of the deceased that were 50% of the assessed value. This wasn't a problem since it involved heirs and relatives. Jonathan found several of these bargain properties were purchased by Byron three months after the original sale. These were at 60% of the assessed value of the properties. The relatives thought they were making a 10% profit. In fact, they were being screwed out of 40% of the property's value.

"It's a rather elegant scheme, isn't it?" Thompson remarked. "It's not clear to me if it's crooked or just underhanded.

"Were all the deaths on the up and up?" I asked.

"I didn't note any problems at the time, but I may take a second look," Thompson replied. "There is a regular pattern here that is a bit inconsistent with natural deaths. How regular is it?"

"It's like clockwork," Jonathan replied. "The sales occurred two weeks after the death unless it occurred on the weekend. The first time it happened it was ten years ago, but the pace of the sales has picked up recently."

Financial schemes aren't my strong suit, but Jonathan and Carl were cautious men. They thought something was amiss. After the meeting broke up, I went by Aunt Edith's house and went through it. It had been well boarded up and was dark inside. I wasn't sure anyone would buy it. If you wanted a haunted house, this was the place for you.

Thompson asked me to dinner and after a depressing hour in Edith's house, I drove to his cabin. His wife was out of town taking care of an elderly relative and the sheriff was on his own. There were a couple cars at the cabin when I got there.

Much to my surprise, Reggie and Juan were there. Reggie was the Sheriff's distant cousin. They had been childhood friends and had moved away at age 12 and drifted apart. During questioning, Thompson discovered Reggie's identity. I had thought they'd have been kicked out of the county but they were working part time for the Sheriff. We had a nice reunion. Thompson was held up at the office and would get here as soon as possible.

Reggie filled me in on the news of the former Resource Management staff. Halsey was now working for Capitol. He was showing them were they had changed markers. "Halsey has a good memory when he's not on the sauce," Reggie explained. "Sean and Halsey hit it off and they are working together. It's big money for Sean so he has a reason to help Halsey keep away from demon Rum. They can't find Mark Jones at all. It was probably a fake name."

"Juan hit it off with the Sheriff big time, so things have settled down here. It turns out the Sheriff never had a son and Juan never had a father. It worked out real nice. Juan likes having a dad; Thompson liked having a son, and they both like the fringe benefits. Juan's hole and Thompson's cock are a perfect fit," Reggie explained. "We're doing yard work for folks and doing pretty well."

"And how is your battle with demon Rum?"

"Not bad," Reggie replied. "Regular sex seems to make the booze less important. Living out here alone seems to appeal to some of the locals. They can drop by and have some fun apart from their wives. As you know, I can take a cock and smile. I've had more fun in the last two months than I had in the previous ten years."

The phone rang inside the cabin and Reggie went to get it. He returned a few minutes later. "It was the Sheriff. There was a pipe bomb in a mailbox. Some guy named Jonathan was hurt. He thinks you might want to come to the hospital."

I jump into my car and raced to the hospital. Jonathan in the operating room. They were trying to save his hand. Carl was sitting in the Emergency Room. He had been cut by flying shrapnel. He looked like shit and was a bit dazed but the doctor said he was okay. I called my Mom and told her what had happened. She got in touch with Graham.

I returned to Carl and talked with him. After leaving the office they had gone back to the County Clerk's office. They had checked a few things there and then went to Jonathan's house. It was a few miles out of town. When Jonathan went to open the mailbox, it exploded. Jonathan got the full force of the blast and his body had protected Carl from the worst of the explosion.

I wanted to go to the house to look over the scene, but Carl was alone. Most of the clerk's staff was at the hospital as were Jonathan's Uncle and Aunt. Jonathan was in critical condition. I assumed they knew about Jonathan and Carl's relationship, but they couldn't quite acknowledge it. I had a cell phone, went out of the hospital, and called Rev. Pettigrew. He said he be right over. I had a message from my Mom saying she and Graham were on their way. I wasn't too happy to have them driving on country roads in the dark, but cousin Buddy was driving them.

Carl was beginning to feel poorly. The shock had numbed the pain, but was wearing off. Pettigrew and Tom, the organist arrived and took him under their wing. The hospital wasn't big and they called in additional staff. Jonathan's wounds were serious. Treating him was using most of the available staff. One of the new nurses saw Carl and called for another doctor. Rev. Pettigrew and Tom stayed with Carl and I went off to find the Sheriff.

Rollie was at the hospital guarding Jonathan. He told me where the house was. I drove and found it easily. It was secluded and there were no neighbors who had a view of the house or the mailbox. The Bomb Squad from Roanoke was on the way. Thompson was guarding the site to insure nothing was moved. Bombs were not in Thompson's areas of specialty.

Jonathan's dog was in the house in a state. It was a small Schnauzer who must have seen the explosion and was distressed. He wouldn't let anyone in the house. I have a way with dogs and was able to calm him down. I got in the house and found his leash. We went on a walk. The dog was well house trained and needed a tree badly. Once we took care of that, we did a circuit of the house.

I don't think Schnauzers' are trackers, but this animal picked up something. He led me to a thicket on the side of the property. I called some Policemen over. They had flashlights and found some broken branches and an older model cell phone.

For some reason I had assumed the bomb had been set off by a mechanical device. The cell phone had been the detonator. Someone had been watching the house waiting for Jonathan. Thompson was overjoyed.

Cell phones can be traced and the bomber may have left other clues at the site.

Mom, Graham and Buddy arrived at 1:00 in the morning. That was when Jonathan got out of surgery. They hadn't been able to save his hand, but they had sewn the rest him back together. They were afraid he had lost his eyes, but they thought they had saved them. The bomb was small, but had been filled with shrapnel. It was a man killer.

Carl was to go into the operating room next. They had essentially duct taped him together immediately after the explosion. They now had to sew him up right. Mom reverted to her calm. Nurse-in-control mode and was helpful for Carl and for Jonathan's friends. One of Jonathan's staff members, a woman named Donna was nearly hysterical.

Donna was a middle-aged woman who must have been a hot woman twenty years earlier. She still dressed in the Dolly Parton style. Perhaps she was naturally a hysteric, but I wondered if something else was going on. I asked Mom to talk to her. Graham was with his son so Mom went to work.

Mom later told me that the hysterics at the side of the deathbed were typically the relatives who had been screw-ups, or had done something bad and needed forgiveness. Graham came out of the hospital room when Carl went into surgery.

"He seems to be doing well," Graham said. "I think he still partially in shock."

"That would be normal. I've been hurt a few times in the course of my work. It can really through you for a loop. I kind of think it comes with the territory for my job. It's not part of an accountant's job description."

"He looks horrible," Graham said.

"I think he looks worse than he is. Cuts look dramatic and are really messy, but they aren't life altering," I explained.

"He's really worried about Jonathan," Graham said. "He's been happier over the last few months than he had been in years. He is normally quite sullen and withdrawn. Was that because of Jonathan?"

"I think they really hit it off," I said.

"It's more than friendship, isn't it?"

"You're relationship with Mom is more than friendship too, isn't it?" I remarked.

"You noticed?"

I smiled. "You don't need to be a detective to see that."

"My late wife was a wonderful woman. When she died, I never guessed I would ever find anyone who could replace her. I didn't know lightening could strike twice."

"Somehow I suspect lightening has only struck your son once," I said.

"He has always been a good boy. He deserves happiness," Graham said. Carl got out of surgery at 3:00; he was heavily sedated. We went to Elizabeth's house. Buddy and I went to Scooter's doublewide. I woke at ten, alone. Buddy left me a note saying he had taken Mom and Graham back to the hospital. Scooter appeared after is morning chores. He took a quick shower and then joined me in bed.

Scooter told me he missed my ball juice and he wanted me just to lay back and let him milk me. Scooter must have been taking lessons. He had always been a good cocksucker, but he was great this morning. He was a dairy man, so he liked the milking thing in general. He told me to relax and let him do the work.

I'm always uneasy about shooting off. Some guys don't like sucking another guy's sperm. I ask before I deposit the cream in a guy's mouth or ass. Scooter loved it and took each load with enthusiasm. I was a little tense the first time I popped but the second and third times were prefect. He had to get back to work. As he got up I managed to snag his cock and with one quick lick, I got him to pop. It was beautiful. I went to the hospital. Graham was with Carl. Mom came over to me and whispered. "Could you get the Sheriff over here?" she asked. "Donna has something she needs to tell him."

Chief Thompson was there in ten minutes. The Sheriff and Donna went to talk. Mom told me what was up. Donna was dating Byron and had hopes of marriage. Donna told him she had been slipping Byron information over the years about property transfers and had personally handled some of the lawyer's personal stuff. She thought Byron was in love with her and would divorce his wife to find true love in her arms. Thompson was disgusted at that outbreak of stupidity. Byron's wife was the daughter and only child of the town's banker. There was no chance true love would trump real cash.

Thompson thought Bryon wasn't a bomber type; he also didn't think he was the kind of man who would watch the scene until the victim appeared and then press the detonator and watch the guy blow up. That took a special kind of person. Thompson had some clear thoughts as to who that might be.

Thompson also told me Carl had acted coolly and bravely. While he was wounded, he tied a tourniquet on Jonathan's arm and called 911. He almost certainly had saved Jonathan's life at the expense of considerable loss of his own blood. I left Thompson at his work and went back to the hospital. Mom and Graham were with Carl and Jonathan's Uncle and Aunt had come by to give them an update on Jonathan's condition.

They were all of the same generation and got along well. Later that evening Mom came into the hall with me and I thanked her for getting Donna to fess up.

"She's not the brightest bulb in the hard ware store, but I don't think she had any idea what was up. When she realized what she had done, she was devastated," Mom said. "Being foolish isn't a crime."

"You can't undo what happened to Jonathan," I said. A big man in a blue suit came up to me. "Are you by any chance Clydesdale?" he asked. I nodded.

"You were described to me, and I figured there couldn't be two of you," he said. "I'm special Agent Travis Walton with the FBI. I'm the agent in charge of this case."

"I'm Clydesdale Noland and this is my mother," I said. We all shook hands.

"Your son is well known in these parts," he said. "I believe it was your sister's death that began to unravel the scheme. I've been working on it for two months and it keeps on getting more convoluted. After some small talk, he asked if we could talk privately.

We went outside. Wythetown was a hard place to be private. Everyone knew about the bombing and wanted to know more. We went to the diner and I asked Andy if we could talk in his apartment. It was no problem.

Walton had been working on the interstate commerce aspect of the case trying to run down the Texas and Oklahoma portions scheme. He had come up with nothing, zip, zero, not a thing. "I've worked a lot of cases like this, but have never found anything," he said. "The Mafia guys are confessing, but the Resource Management people are elusive. I was beginning to think we were barking up the wrong tree. When I heard about Byron Semple Esquire, I began to wonder. Is it possible the real center of the scheme is here and the western corporation is a dummy, intended to divert attention?"

"How nothing is anything in your investigation of Resource Management?" I asked.

"The officers of the corporation do not seem to exist," Travis said. "The lawyer who filed for the incorporation papers died a year and a half before the filing date. I guess someone had his stationary."

"I wonder if Byron has any friends or relatives in the west." I asked. "Byron filed the papers in Virginia. He didn't mention the connection in association with Edith's death. That could be just an error in judgment. Somehow, a misjudgment or error would have to be really bad to justify a bombing. Byron must know Jonathan well. It seems to me you would need to have a pretty compelling reason to blow up a friend."

We talked for a while and I noticed Travis took a few glances at my crotch. He had said I was well known in these parts. I wondered if I was known for more than my detective skills. Travis mentioned he had talked with Captain Donnan of the arson squad. We had dinner at the diner. It was a slow day and we talked with Andy. I noticed Travis and Andy hit it off. When Andy closed the diner at 8:00, he asked us upstairs for some special deserts.

Andy took a shower after his day in the hot kitchen. Andy had told me he wasn't gay; he just liked sex with men. Apparently, he had great gaydar and he knew Travis was interested. Andy dried off in view and Travis was all but drooling. Andy pulled on some shorts and produced some spectacular Greek pastries. Travis wasn't gourmet and he had never had anything like Andy's pastries. He loved it. Travis was going to Roanoke to get a hotel room. Andy offered Travis his couch.

I know when three's a crowd, so I went off the Scooter's double wide and left Travis and Andy to their own devices. Mom and Graham must have still been at the hospital, since their car wasn't at Elizabeth's. I went to Scooter's and found he had a few friends over. Inside Tom, Festus and my friends, troopers Bull Morris and Boomer Smith, were waiting. Rollie was questioning the suspects at the police station. Scooter told me he teamed with Sue, the woman who questioned me after the aborted robbery at the diner. Scooter explained, "Rollie's the good cop; Sue's the bad cop."

I had some fun with these guys at Rollie's birthday party weeks earlier. This time they were ready, cocked and loaded. When I walked in the door, Boomer began to take his shirt off. Boomer had been following Bull's lead at Rollie's party. Tonight he was the starter. It turned into one of those parties when you walk in the door, strip and start screwing.

It was Boomer's birthday and he was getting the same presents Rollie got at his party. I fed Boomer my cock and held his legs open as the other men fucked him. They had graded the cocks by size so Tom, Festus, Scooter and then Bull fucked him. Boomer was a good sport, but he really enjoyed Bull Morris. A cock can only be so bad in my estimation, but it can be great when it's attached to a man you love. I didn't know if Troopers Morris and Smith could admit they loved each other, but I could feel it.

I was the final fucker. Boomer and Morris got in the 69 position. This left Bull with a front row seat overlooking my cock as I worked it into his lover's ass. Boomer liked it well enough, but Morris loved it. Boomer's asshole was swollen and a bit battered by now. Morris pulled it open with his fingers and man cream drooled out. That was too much for me to resist, so I pushed my cock in deep.

As it turned out, there wasn't room in Boomer's ass for my cock and four men's cum. My first push was a hard thrust and the man juices squirted out. It squirted into my bush and then dripped on my hairy ball sack. I was coated. Morris went crazy as he alternated between sucking Boomer's meat and licking up the semen.

When I said good sex can be messy, it was never messier than this. Boomer shot off in Morris's mouth as I shot my load into his quivering ass. I pulled and lay on the bed, exhausted. Festus and Tom gave my cock and balls a good tongue bath. Things calmed down after this and we talked.

Two murders within two months was a big event in a small town like Wytheville. No one wanted Aunt Edith to die the way she did, but had she died in her bed no one would have cared much. Jonathan had been the clerk for 30 years and was a popular man. Boards of Supervisors and County managers came and went, but Jonathan was there keeping things working in the county. He struck me as being prissy, but he was a good clerk and was helpful to anyone who needed help. He had taken care of his widowed mother, and there was general agreement he deserved a better mother than he got.

No one would say it out loud, but many were glad he had finally found a friend. After taking care of his mother he deserved a friend. Jonathan was always prim and proper, and it seemed to be almost a desecration that he was ripped to pieces by the bomb.

There were suspects. The Rafferty family was nasty and permanently at war with the county. They took a generous view of property lines and felt you gained ownership by regular trespassing. Needless to say, Jonathan had a different view. They had a very public feud. They attempted to attack him once but were caught, mid attack by Sheriff Thompson's predecessor, Sheriff Mills. Mills wasn't a firm believer in the Trial by Jury thing. He liked to do his punishing during the arrest.

Another man, Donzell Duke, was way too interested in explosives. As a teenager, he blew up the boy's room at the high School. Donzell had joined the Marines, but was been kicked out for emotional issues. The Marines introduced him to high-powered explosives. That wasn't good. We talked for a while and then had a second playtime.

I had a nice long fuck session with Festus, and let the birthday boy take a ride in my ass. Bull joined him and the two men had a good time. When Boomer gets really close to shooting in my hole, Bull rear-ended him and we had a triple orgasm. The party broke up and I actually got some sleep.

It was as if the circus had come to town the next day. We had ATF agents. State Troopers and the Bomb Squad as well as a Postal Inspector. I met with him and gave him the outline of the case. Chief Thompson was too busy. The Post Office really dislikes bombs in mailboxes. The Inspector, a tall thin guy named Elmer Farrar was mild mannered and quiet. He was also good at what he did and had an encyclopedic knowledge of pipe bombs. He also knew of every similar case in Virginia.

Pipe bombs were at the lowest level of the bomb squads concerns, but at the top of Elmer's. Some people think they are jokes, but losing a hand is no minor wound. The Bomb people had a chemical analysis of the bomb. Elmer looked it over. He said most of the ingredients were common; one chemical was unusual. That was important.

Bombs can be made of materials you can easily find. The presence of this chemical indicated the bomber was more than a crank. It was also the sort of thing that could make a search warrant valuable. While you could say some things, such as fertilizer, had legitimate uses, this chemical was useful in explosives.

Chief Thompson was narrowing his list of potential bombers and was moving up to the search warrant level. This was good news for him.

Elmer was looking for a place to stay. The motel situation in Wythetown was poor. It was essentially two hours to the nearest viable motel. I was at Scooter's doublewide; Mom was at Elizabeth's. I called Tom, the Episcopalian organist, and asked if he could offer his house as a place for the investigators to crash. He was more than willing. Jonathan was a pillar of the Episcopalian Church and they went into overdrive to help Jonathan any way they could.

Tom's house was the former rectory and was large with multiple bedrooms. It was a mile from the bombsite. Tom is a short, intense hairy man. I wouldn't say he was effeminate, but it wouldn't take a trained investigator to know he was gay. Some of the men decided to make the trip to Roanoke or Martinsburg to spend the night. Others set of camp in the former Rectory. I guess you could say they were the more open-minded ones. Elmer was one of the open-minded ones.

You don't need to be gay to like a blowjob once and a while. Some of the guys understood Tom wouldn't mind a taste of Bomb Squad semen. Bomb Squad and ATF men are up tight guys. The prospect of being blown to kingdom come on a daily basis isn't conducive to a relaxed approach to life. Nothing is more relaxing for a man than a complete change of reproductive juices. I think when you suck the sperm from a guy's balls, they go in overdrive to replace and refill the missing fluids.

I've suspected this is why you get sleepy after you shoot off. Now, I'm pretty sure your balls are the gift that keeps on giving. Somehow I'm positive your balls are never happier that when they are churning out little pollywogs to repopulate the earth. Your balls never get sore. I've had some really good nights when I've shot off five or six times. When I woke up the next morning I'd be drained, but I'm still hard as a rock and fully recharged.

Elmer, Travis and a bomb guy named Henry stayed at the Rectory for several days. Bull and Boomer dropped by too. Tom, Rev. Pettigrew, Dan were at the house most of the time. They knew how to unwind too tightly wound policemen. You might be surprised at how many straight policemen dropped by.

I was interviewing contactors to work on my Aunt's house when Tom dropped by. He told me I might drop by the Rectory that evening. He said they could use another top. Somehow, when thoughts turn to sex, thoughts also turn toward me. I don't think of myself as being oversexed, although I don't seem to avoid sex when the potential pops up. I explained this to my friend Mark and he didn't say a word. He laughed a lot, but he didn't say a word.

That afternoon I did have a little fun with one of the contractors. Billy Baker was a nice guy, a bit short, but well built. He did many renovations and thought the house was in pretty good shape except for the soot. He suggested we clean it up, paint and polish it up, but not do a full renovation. "Sell it as is at a good price and let the new owner put in the new bathrooms and kitchen," he suggested. "Maybe a home owner could do it himself or a contractor could renovate it on spec."

We got along well, and he knew his stuff. He told me he had some financial setbacks recently, so he'd need some cash up front to get underway. Billy said he'd been taken to the cleaners by a shyster lawyer and was just getting back on his feet. The lawyer turned out to be none other than Byron Q. R. Semple. Bryon hired Billy to renovate his house, told him to do considerable extra work and then refused to pay.

"How much were you in the hole for?" I asked.

"$40,000.00 plus or minus," Billy said. "I know I was stupid. He seemed like such a nice guy, and we got along so well, I believed he was legit. I also found out my wife had married me for better or for worse, except for the worse part. Last year was a bad year."

"Did you go to court?"

"I tried, but he had a pal who lied for him. If you ever run into a guy named Donzell Duke run as far away as fast as you can," Billy added.

With that comment, I decided to hire Billy on the spot. Billy wore tight jeans and they were well worn. He was nicely equipped. I guessed he was straight, but I liked the scenery. My jeans were not as tight, but more worn and Billy had noticed. He wasn't obvious, but he noticed. We went to his apartment to work on a contract. As I drove to the apartment, I called the Chief and told him about Donzell Duke. He knew exactly what that meant.

At the house, I had brushed against Billy and he didn't react. At his apartment, he wrote up a simple contact and we signed it. We had a beer to seal the contract. He brushed against me this time. His apartment had a bed, a small table, a kitchen chair and a twenty-year-old TV. "I guess your wife cleaned you out," I said.

"If they still had gold fillings for teeth she's have taken them," he said. "To tell you the truth things between us had been going downhill for a while. I'm not sure I ever would have been successful enough for her." Billy was looking at my crotch. "Have you been married?"

"Everyone thinks I'm too ugly to get married," I replied. "To tell you the truth I'm not much into women." He rubbed his crotch. "Do you think we might pool our resources and have some fun?"

"I've never done that before," he said. He cock was getting hard and I could see it in his too tight jeans. He realized that. "I guess I'm a bit curious. Are you gay?"

"I sure am, but I'm not looking for true love, just some fun," I said. Billy and I had a good time. Billy was shy until I got his cock in my mouth. He knew a good thing when he found it. Billy had been in a sexual drought for a year and he was needed some real sex bad. I had no plans to push him anywhere he didn't want to go. I had guessed reciprocity would be a step too far for him.

Billy was polite, grateful and appreciative. He pulled his jeans down and I sucked him; he shot off quickly. I told him get on the bed and we could do it again. He was more than willing, we stripped naked, and we got on the bed

"What's your recharge time?" I asked.

"When I was younger it was ten minutes. I don't know what it is now."

"Do you mind if I do a little investigating on that subject?" I asked. "I like the cream and unless you have other plans for it, I wouldn't mind draining you."

"Not at all; it was good. I've got a hair trigger, sorry about that." We talked as I fondled his balls. Billy was dirty blond with a nice mat of hair in his chest and a well-defined treasure trail to his bush. He was uncut and had an easy to deep throat, average size cock. I wasn't sure he would reciprocate. This was new to him and I don't like to push a guy beyond his limit.

Billy asked me if he had to suck me. I told him no; it wasn't required. More often than not, this answer seems to take the pressure off. When the pressure lowers, the lust grows. I sucked him again and he popped a second time. It was a nice gully washer of an orgasm. Billy must have been saving up. I asked him if he could do a third. He wasn't sure, but he'd like to try.

He leaned over and licked my cock during the interlude between his second and third climaxes. Billy got downright enthusiastic when I got him in the sixty-nine position. He was really relaxed for the third orgasm. He fell asleep. I got dressed and went to the Chief. Billy's information about Donzell was the missing link. Donzell had prior arrests and was on probation for DUI. Rollie and Sue were doing the good cop-bad cop routine on him and it worked like a charm.

Part 14

As soon as Donzell cracked, warrants went out for Byron. All hell broke out that evening. There were raids on Donzell Duke's farm and Byron's house. Since there was murder, arson and a bombing associated with the case the police took no chances. Donzell could have booby trapped his house and Bryon's house for that matter.

At 4:30, Byron saw the police cruisers drive up. He knew what that meant. He locked himself in the house and took his wife hostage. It was a bad scene, but there was one good aspect to it. Trooper Fluffy was on the scene and when Bryon tried to make a run for it with the gun at his wife's head, Fluffy went into action. Like Sid before him, Byron didn't see the animal coming. Fluffy wasn't a barker; he was a stealth dog. Byron still had the gun in his hand as Fluffy tried to detach the hand from his arm.

Bluto grabbed Byron's wife and got her to safety. This gave Fluffy some quality time with Byron. The gun went off once, but the bullet went wild. He hadn't been able to give Sid the treatment he deserved. Byron's arrest made up for that. Fluffy was a happy dog. The town police got Byron. Rollie and Sue were the arresting officers.

That night Chief Thompson asked me to come by his cabin. "I'm having a little get together. Everyone's going home tomorrow," he said. "This is sort of a farewell party." When I got there Elmer, the Postal Inspector, Travis, the ATF agent, and Henry, a bomb guy were talking with Rollie, Scooter and Bull. Boomer was guarding Byron, as the lawyer was duct taped together at the hospital. The hospital staff had done the same with Jonathan and Carl earlier in the week and Byron wasn't high on their list of favorite people. Thompson told me he wanted to insure nothing happened to him before the trial. Bluto was filling out forms for Fluffy. Technically Fluffy wasn't supposed to do to Byron what he did. Since Byron was still armed, it was justifiable, but Bluto wanted to make sure Fluffy's record was clean.

We were a happy group. Andy appeared with a sandwich tray and there was some non-communion wine provided by Rev. Pettigrew. The Reverend was on his way back to the hospital to see Jonathan and then was going to help Byron's wife. Byron had dislocated her shoulder when he tried to escape. Rev. Pettigrew wasn't my idea of a leader of men, but he was where he needed to be when he was needed.

It amazes me how many lives a crooked money making scheme can screw up. Edith was dead, Jonathan maimed and a slew of people were terrorized. I can't figure out how anyone could have thought it was worth it. Sid and Byron would spend the rest of their lives in jail. By contrast, the firefighters, police and assorted investigators were working to hold things together and make things good again. It is so easy for one or two bad men to screw things up, and so hard for the good guys to get things right again.

We talked and traded stories and tried to fill in the gaps in the case. Our understanding of what was going on was correct except for one important detail. Resource Management was a franchise operation. That hadn't occurred to me. The brains behind the scheme were in Texas, but they sold the rights to different areas to locals. They took care of the field operations. There were individual groups in West Virginia, California, Pennsylvania and Oklahoma all trying the same swindle on abandoned oil fields and coalmines. The Virginia group owned by Byron was going after Capitol Exploration. The brains took the Texas franchise for themselves. This was a much bigger operation and focused on oil, of course. Apparently, the company they were scamming was a much bigger operation then Capitol. This company didn't like it at all and weren't the forgiving type. Resource Management officers had all met with unfortunate accidents.

That explained why Travis had been unable to find them. They were dead and buried, dissolved, or burned. Byron's little piece of the action continued on as an independent operation. Apparently, Bryon noticed the mysterious disappearance of the Texas branch, and that was why he registered the corporation in Virginia. He wanted it to look like an independent company. Byron also had an unsuspected nasty streak. The nasty streak took the form of using Donzell Duke as his enforcer. Bryon had represented Donzell in most of his scrapes with the law and they got to be friends of a sort. No one in town guessed they were working together.

Donzell was a paranoid sadist and had been Byron's chief connection to Sid. Sid's sadism was drug enhanced. Donzell's was natural and 24/7. While bombs were Donzell's chief pride and joy, he had a sideline making designer drugs. He provided Sid with his mood enhancers.

It was a warm night and the small cabin was crowded. It got hot and Chief Thompson suggested a dip in the lake. No one even tried the, "I don't have any swimming trunks line." Everyone was ready.

It turned out Elmer and Henry had plans for me. They had met at Tom's house and had hit it off big time. Tom, the church organist, had joined in the festivities and had let slip some information about my personal endowment that intrigued both men. I like to think of sex as being a spur of the moment thing, but I guess if you're into bombs, you prefer more planning and fewer surprises.

Elmer had a nice white snake gangling from his groin. Under his clothes, he was a muscle builder. I hadn't guessed that. Henry was a bland, Joe Average kind of guy. He was smooth and had average endowment. Travis was beefy, and hairy.

There was one big surprise. Elmer, Henry and Travis were semi virgins. While they had sex, they knew man sex only as quickies. Until they came to Wythetown, they had never experienced get naked and get in bed sex with another man. Their stay at the rectory with Tom provided a safe place to experiment with man sex for the first time in their lives. It helped that all the men in the house were like spirits. They were all in law enforcement and shared common experiences and fears. Apparently, their experiments were successful.

I think being out is preferable for most men, but that can be hard especially in law enforcement. I had discovered you run the risk of losing your job. It's hard and sometimes impossible for a forty or fifty year old man to turn on a dime. These men were all straight arrows and devoted to their jobs; everyone needs love and affection sometime and that goes double for closeted police. They had guns. It's much better to shoot their sperm into a buddies mouth than to fire a gun.

Tom, the organist, had been doing some missionary work. He wanted to save men from sexual repression. Andy also had been doing his part. Andy and Tom were beefy hairballs. When they passed out male hormones, they both got a double dose. It would be hard to believe Tom and Andy were the same species as the hairdressers and queens you see in the movies. Travis had fallen for Andy big time. Andy was somewhat new to the scene, but he loved a cock in his ass. That was good for Travis.

Tom introduced them to bottoming. The organist had a thin six incher and it was just about the perfect cock for a first fuck. It didn't hurt and was long enough to reach the prostate. I soon discovered Tom had been opening up the men to the possibilities. None of this was true love, with the possible exception of Travis and Andy, but it was good.

The water in the lake was warm, but still cool enough to be refreshing. As we played in the water the sun set and it got dark. There was no moon that night.

I was on the grass after a swim when Elmer came by to talk. He also dangled his snake near my mouth. I rose to the bait and snagged the tip of his foreskin. I then sucked it into my mouth. Elmer had seemed all business, but once my tongue was inside the foreskin, I got a nice taste of his ball juices. He had been oozing. Elmer was a quiet man, but he cock was into it. He straddled me and fed me the entire organ. His cock was thin and long. It also bent downward, so it was designed to tickle my tonsils. As I sucked Elmer, someone went after my cock.

For some reason I thought it was Henry. When I finally got a look, it was Travis. Henry was with Bull and Andy. Travis couldn't get much of my cock into his mouth, but he got more enthusiastic as he worked on it. I managed to rotate and let Elmer suck me while I nursed on Travis. Travis had a beer can style type cock and his balls were all but breweries of rich and tasty man juices. You can be the strong impassive and silent type cop, but there is no way your cock can be impassive.

As far as I can tell, your cock can go from asleep to being ready to party in 30 seconds. If something or someone turns you on your cock will be ready, even if you're trying to be responsible and avoid temptation. As far as I could tell, no one here was trying to avoid temptations at all. I've never avoided temptation, but I guess it is possible. No one at the Chief's cabin was successful resisting temptation either.

It was a relaxing evening. After the stress of the investigation, it was good to lay back and let nature take its course. It ended with a good exchange of sperm and a lot of fun.

I went home the next day and got back to my day job at Clydesdale & Company. Travis called me a few times. He was looking into the disappearance of the leadership of Resource Management. Travis was firmly of the belief that punishment was the duty of the government, not corporations. He found four people associated with Resource had vanished without a trace and was unhappy about that.

Jonathan and Carl were living at Graham's house and my Mom nursed them. Mom was retired, but she could never resist the chance to help and her nursing skills were as good as ever. She was more worried about the psychological problems that the bombing might have been generated. Oddly, my Mom was the thoughtful and considerate mother Jonathan never had. His mother had been a terror. Mom was firm but fair, but she was not prone to be tolerant of self-pity. Jonathan finally had the mother he deserved. All was well.

Jonathan and Carl also did well. Graham and Mom accepted their relationship and that was good especially for Carl. He had lived in fear his father would discover his sexual preference. As Jonathan got better, the situation evolved. Jonathan wasn't blind, but his eyesight had greatly deteriorated. There was no way he could resume his job as clerk. The four of them worked things out well.

A few months later, I made another trip back to Wytheville to see Aunt Edith's house. Billy had fixed it up and it looked great. He lived there during the construction process and the house looked better than I dreamed it could. There was no trace of the fire, or of the dirty old wallpaper. All the old curtains and dusty drapes were gone and the place was sun filled and cheerful.

Billy had brought the work in $3,000.00 under the price he gave me. We went to have dinner at Andy's diner. I was going to head back to

Richmond that night, but Billy said I could stay at the house. Billy was hesitant about asking me to stay. I knew what that meant. I went back to Aunt Edith's house.

Maybe there are ghosts, but Billy's renovation had banished them. New paint and sunlight made it a new place. We sat at Billy little kitchen table and had a few beers. Billy was nervous.

"I'm tired. I need to get to bed," I said.

"I'm afraid I only have one bed here, I have a sleeping bag," Billy said.

"We can share if you want to," I suggested.

Billy looked at me. "I'd like that a lot." We went to bed. It was a very good night.

About the Author

Bob Archman lives in rural Virginia in the shadow of the Blue Ridge and finds writing gay themed adventure fantasies and a pleasant way to spend time. He is interested in older, mature men many of whom aren't conventionally regarded as attractive. He discovered many years ago not even gay men can stay young forever. Most aren't flamboyant hairdressers, florists or interior decorators as is often portrayed in the media. Bob is interested in stories about everyday working guys who don't fit the stereotyped images of gay men.

Bob Archman is also the Author of *Clydedale & Company, Clydesdale Goes to the Hunt* and *The Cave of the Blue Bear*. Available from Amazon.com, TheNazcaPlainsCorp.com or your local bookstore.

Clydesdale
& COMPANY

Archman

CLYDESDALE & COMPANY

A
BONER
BOOK

A NOVEL BY
Bob Archman

Archman

CLYDESDALE GOES TO THE HUNT

A
BONER
BOOK

Clydesdale
GOES TO THE HUNT

A NOVEL BY
Bob Archman

The Cave of the Blue Bear

Archman

The Cave of the Blue Bear

a novel by
Bob Archman

www.ingramcontent.com/pod-product-compliance
Lightning Source LLC
Chambersburg PA
CBHW051147260626
47170CB00005B/2000